BRATFEST AT TIFFANY'S

CLIQUE novels by Lisi Harrison:

THE CLIQUE

BEST FRIENDS FOR NEVER

REVENGE OF THE WANNABES

INVASION OF THE BOY SNATCHERS

THE PRETTY COMMITTEE STRIKES BACK

DIAL L FOR LOSER

IT'S NOT EASY BEING MEAN

SEALED WITH A DISS

BRATFEST AT TIFFANY'S

If you like THE CLIQUE, you may also enjoy:

Bass Ackwards and Belly Up by Elizabeth Craft and Sarah Fain

Secrets of My Hollywood Life by Jen Calonita

Haters by Alisa Valdes-Rodriguez

Betwixt by Tara Bray Smith

BRATFEST AT TIFFANY'S

A CLIQUE NOVEL BY
LISI HARRISON

LITTLE, BROWN AND COMPANY
New York Boston

Poppy

Little, Brown and Company
Hachette Book Group USA
237 Park Avenue, New York, NY 10017
For more of your favorite series, go to www.pickapoppy.com

First Edition: February 2008

Cover design by Andrea C. Uva
Cover and author photos by Roger Moenks

Produced by Alloy Entertainment
151 West 26th Street, New York, NY 10001

ISBN: 978-0-316-00680-4

10 9 8 7 6 5 4 3 2 1
CWO
Printed in the United States of America

For Jesse Fox, who was with me every day while I wrote this.

BRIARWOOD–OCTAVIAN COUNTRY DAY SCHOOL
THE CAFÉ
Tuesday, September 8th
7:23 A.M.

ALL STUDENTS MUST KEEP OUT UNTIL 8 A.M. NO EXCEPTIONS.

"Puh-lease!" Massie Block ripped the sign off the frosted glass doors of the Café.

"What are you *doing*?" gasped Claire Lyons, searching the empty hall for witnesses.

"It's a piece of poster board, Kuh-laire." Massie kicked it aside. "What's it gonna do, paper-cut us to death?"

Claire giggle-shrugged.

"Now get serious. This mission is top priority." Massie gripped the door's silver pump handle, with its back-to-school shine, and then paused to admire her deeply tanned, Chanel No. 19–scented hands.

Their rich butterscotch hue said, "Why, yes, my summer *was* perfect. I feel confident, relaxed, and on top of my game. I'm ready for the new year. Ready for the Briarwood boys to move into OCD. Ready to meet *and* defeat the new crop of seventh-graders. Ready to dominate—eighth-grade alpha style."

But if asked, her heart would have told a very different story. . . .

More than anything, Massie wanted to collapse on the freshly waxed floor, curl into the fetal position, and roll straight into the school shrink's office. Once comfortable, she'd tell Dr. Baum how she'd been stressing about this day since mid-May. How she was secretly afraid of the Briarwood boys. How her alpha status was in jeopardy. And how she was on high alert, in extreme danger of becoming an LBR.

"What exactly is an LBR?" Dr. Baum would ask, burgundy Montblanc poised above her yellow legal pad.

"Loser beyond repair."

"Ahhh." She would make note. "And why are you so afraid of *boys*?"

"I'm not afraid of *boys*," Massie would snap. "Just the Briarwood ones. Well, actually the soccer players."

Dr. Baum would remove her rectangular black plastic Lens-Crafters frames and re-cross her hose-covered legs. "Go on."

Massie would inhale deeply and then continue.

"Last year, the Pretty Committee won this key to a bomb shelter in the basement of OCD. Inside, there was a flat-screen that linked to the boys' sensitivity-training class at Briarwood. We watched it a few times and heard all of their secret confessions. . . ."

Dr. Baum's thin, coral pink lips would part, but knowing it was her job to listen and not judge people for spying, she'd nod attentively and continue speed-writing.

"After that we kind of started acting like freaks around our crushes because we thought we knew what they were thinking, even though it turns out we really didn't, so they all dumped us at Skye Hamilton's end-of-the-year costume party."

Flipping to a new sheet of paper, the shrink would continue scribbling at a wrist-snapping pace.

"And it's not so much being *dumped* that bugs me," Massie would explain, "because it's kind of alpha to have a bunch of ex-crushes. It shows you have experience."

"So what *is* it that bugs you?" Dr. Baum would finally allow herself to ask.

Massie would run her hand across the pea green chenille fabric on the worn couch, searching for the best way to explain.

"It bugs me how the girls at OCD are so super-excited to have boys at our school."

Dr. Baum would stop writing, look up, and put on her LensCrafters. Her head would tilt slightly to the right, and her black, overgrown brows would collide in confusion.

"Be-*cause*," Massie would sigh, "if they're as excited as I know they're going to be, the boys will be upgraded to 'beyond popular' status, which automatically makes *them* the new alphas. And if the new alphas don't like *us*—which they don't—the Pretty Committee will be downgraded to LBRs. And if I become an LBR . . ." She'd look up at the white stucco ceiling, reversing the direction of her hot tears. "And if I become an LBR, I'll have to move to Canada and start over and . . ." Massie would look at the doctor intensely. "And Glossip Girl doesn't ship to Canada." She'd grab a Puffs Plus from the wicker box on the end table and blow. "No one does."

At this point Dr. Baum would immediately put down her

notes, buzz her secretary, and insist she cancel all appointments for the rest of the year so she could devote all of her time to this very serious crisis. . . .

Hence, Massie's early-morning decision to hyper-gloss.

The idea was to quadruple the weight of her lips, transforming them into an impenetrable wall. That way, her insecurities would be trapped inside her body, unable to escape. Better they stay churning and burning in the pit of her stomach than make themselves known on this crucial day, where first impressions could make or break the entire year.

"Are you sure we need to do this *now*?" Claire's desperate whine forced Massie back to reality.

"More than sure." Massie reached into her Be & D silver-and-black Venus bowler bag and pulled out a purple glitter–covered placard. She slapped it into Claire's clammy hands.

Claire lifted her canvas beige bucket hat and scanned the glistening script with her wide blue eyes. "Table eighteen reserved for the Pretty Committee?"

"That's what it says." Massie beamed. The shiny, swirly letters were symbolic of her secret pledge—to sparkle and shine every day in the eighth grade.

Over the weekend, she'd ransacked the Westchester Mall, and bought up anything and everything that reflected light. But now, as the bright morning sun flooded the vacant halls of Briarwood–Octavian Country Day, Massie's long-sleeved indigo sequin Tory Burch top suddenly reminded her of a tacky *Dancing with the Stars* contestant. And that made her snippier than Katie Holmes's hairdresser in 2007.

"Kuh-laire!" she huffed. "Eighteen is *our* table. I don't want some LBR seventh-grader or a pack of Briarwood boys to claim it. Do you?"

Claire knit her blond brows, which looked whiter than usual against her sun-soaked skin. "Why don't I just wait here, so when they open the doors, I'll be the first one in?" She glanced over her shoulder and checked the big white clock above a BOYS "R" US banner the student council had spray-painted on a white Frette sheet.

"Um, are you my favorite Chinese takeout dish?" Massie tossed her long dark bangs past her gold-dusted cheekbones.

"No, why?"

"Then why act all gung ho?"

"I'm not." Claire reddened. "I just don't understand why I have to break into the Café and risk getting in trouble on my first day back."

Massie twirled the purple hair streak below her right ear, which she'd dyed during her summer stint in Southampton. If anyone asked, she'd say a Parisian fashion insider had entrusted her with this soon-to-be-international trend. It was much easier than explaining the truth. And a lot more believable.

"We're not *breaking in*." Massie air-quoted Claire. "This is *our* school. *Our* Café. *Our* right!" She hiked up her stylishly slouchy charcoal gray satin knee-length shorts. "Why should *we* be punished because the rooftop wave pool at Briarwood imploded? It's not our fault the entire school is flooded, is it?"

Claire opened her mouth to respond, but Massie quickly cut her off.

"Smell that?" She lifted her tiny ski-slope nose and sniffed. "Paint fumes. The number-one cause of red, itchy eyes. And look. . . ." Her head tilted left, toward the blue stick figure that had been superglued to the door of her favorite bathroom. "Say goodbye to the only mirror in school opposite a window. From now on, we'll be glossing under fluorescents. Which, by the way, will make us look like Kermit the minute our tans fade."

Claire surrender-sighed.

"Now let's move. The girls are waiting outside." Once again, Massie leaned against the silver door handle, and after a single pump, they were in.

"Eh. Ma. Gawd," she gasped.

Claire removed her bucket hat. "What *is* all this?"

They stood in awe, gazing at the Café, which had been transformed into a massive, sun-drenched greenhouse. The new walls were made of glass, and the room's perimeter was lined with mini vegetable gardens framed by low white picket fences. The gardens sprouted ripe red tomatoes, carrots, scallions, peas, cucumbers, and fresh herbs. Rows of new bamboo tables and chairs displayed photos of the happily wrinkled local Westchester artisans who had crafted them. The Starbucks kiosk had been replaced by a charming, old-fashioned stagecoach. It stocked skin-clarifying Borba water (imported from Hong Kong) and drinkable low-fat yogurt guaranteed to speed up hair growth (head only) and increase shine in less than a week. Quaint country chalkboard signs listed the day's freshest produce (edamame and carrots) and the breakfast specials (buttermilk pancakes with chicken sausages, organic eggs Benedict, granola with locally grown fruit), lunch specials (mac 'n' cheese sprinkled with nitrate-free bacon, free-range-turkey burgers, pizza with fresh tomatoes and mozzarella), and desserts (protein-packed chocolate brownies, calorie-burning mint-chip ice-cream cake, tooth-whitening lollipops).

No more steel bars, plastic trays, or orange heat lamps. The Café had become a fabulously ah-dorable, eco-friendly farmer's market gone twenty-first century.

Claire fanned her flushed cheeks with the RESERVED FOR placard. "This is totally—"

"Lame!" Massie barked.

"Huh?"

"How could they do this to me?" Massie gripped her roiling stomach. "I feel like someone replaced my entire wardrobe with, with . . . with *yours*."

Claire rolled her eyes.

"I've been violated."

"How? It's ten times nicer than—"

"The old Café was *mine.* The pine-scented wood, the shortcut to the sushi bar, the Picassos my grandmother donated—I *knew* that place. And now it feels like it belongs to someone else." Massie tugged her purple hair streak. "Someone who loves Birkenstocks and political bumper stickers."

"But—"

"All the more reason to claim our table." Massie cracked her knuckles for the first time in her life. "We need to send the message that things are going to stay the same." She elbow-nudged Claire. "Now will you puh-lease go do it already."

"Fine." Claire shot Massie an *if-I-get-in-trouble-it's-all-your-fault* look. To which Massie responded with a *stop-being-so-pathetically-dramatic* glare. After another sharp exhale, Claire made a run for it.

If anything, Massie still had control over her friend. But whether she still had control over anyone else at the brand-new BOCD remained to be seen.

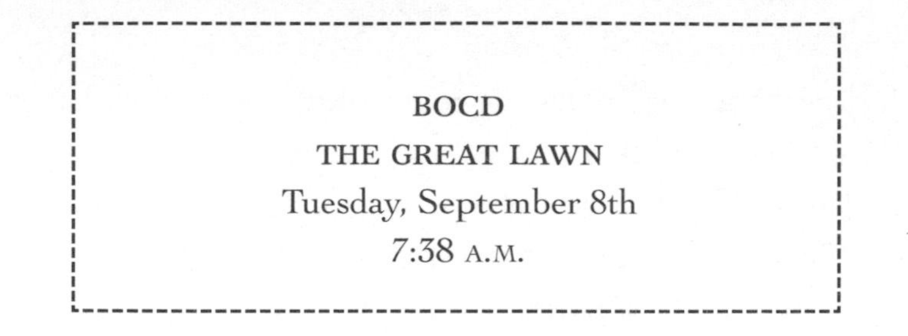

BOCD
THE GREAT LAWN
Tuesday, September 8th
7:38 A.M.

Massie slid on her oversize gold D&G sunglasses and descended upon the Great Lawn to regroup with the Pretty Committee after their summer apart.

"Look at all these boys," Claire panted, scurrying to keep up with Massie's frenzied pace. "They're everywhere."

"A total infestation," Massie hissed at a pack of eighth-grade BMX-ers who skidded by on their muddy black dirt bikes. They dropped their rides on the grass, unclipped their sticker-covered helmets, and shuffled off to greet the rest of their sludge-brothers, who were slouched on the stone stairs below the school's entrance. When a gaggle of Paris-wannabes made their way up the steps, the boys tilted their heads, hoping to see up their skirts. There was no way they actually saw anything, but they snicker-punched one another as if they had.

"We *never* dressed like that in the seventh grade." Massie sneered at the girls' display of bright fuchsia, turquoise, and tangerine ultra-mini halter dresses and lace-up espadrille wedges. "Um, I thought we left Orlando last week."

"Hey!" Claire smacked her playfully on the arm.

"Sorry, but it's true. They dress like your Florida friends," Massie said unapologetically. "I mean ex–Florida friends."

She managed a glossy smile in case anyone was watching them. "Relaxed confidence" was proving hard to pull off since no one—not the pervy bikers, the lowly seventh-graders, or the eighth-grade LBRs—had yet stopped to admire her. Not her shimmering outfit. Not her grown-out bangs. Not the royal purple hair streak below her right ear.

Nuh-*thing*!

It was as though everyone suddenly had a brutal case of social amnesia, and all knowledge of her being this year's alpha-alpha had been deleted from their memories. Were girls so easily distracted by boys? And were boys really so easily attracted to girls with horrific style? A visit to *CosmoGirl*'s FAQ archive was a must as soon as she got home.

Massie stepped onto the cold, dew-covered grass, which poked at her paraffin-waxed feet and most likely stained the leather on her black snakeskin Prada sandals. "This place is so over," she grumbled as she zigzagged through clusters of overdressed, borderline tacky bodies invading *her* lawn.

"Huh?" Claire hurried to keep up, leaving a trail of baby powder–scented deodorant in the wake of her warming pits.

The sun was getting stronger by the minute. Instead of stopping to recharge her tan, Massie wished the ah-nnoyingly cheerful blue sky would cloud over and deliver a cool taste of fall—something to remind her that the Summer of Stress (SOS) was officially over.

But the universe sent a very different message.

It came in the form of a semi-cute, green ski cap–wearing, guitar case–carrying boy, who passed them and smiled.

At *Claire*!

Claire shy-grinned, then lowered her head.

Had the entire world gone mad? Were mass-produced canvas bucket hats and overbleached blondes "in" now that the boys had arrived?

Trying to see her friend from Semi-Cute's perspective, Massie side-glanced at Claire, who *did* look good. For her.

The straight, shoulder-length white-blond hair that in the winter framed her ghostly complexion like limp spaghetti on a hard-boiled egg looked radiant against her tanned, cashew-colored skin. Her light blue eyes glistened like sea glass, and her waxy ChapStick had been replaced (thanks to Massie) with a frosty shade of Be Rosy lip quencher. Even her outfit was semi-decent: a woven long-sleeved cream-colored cotton shirt, fitted olive-colored knee-length Dâ-Nang cargos, and gold Sigerson Morrison gladiator sandals—a gift from Massie if Claire promised to toss her stinky summer Keds, which of course she had.

"There they are." Claire pointed to the middle of the crowded lawn.

"What? Who?" Massie's stomach dip-clenched. Was Derrington in range? Were the soccer guys with him? She had spent months wondering how their first post-breakup encounter would go. Would he beg for forgiveness? Act like nothing had happened? Publicly snub her? There were endless ways for this confrontation to play out. And surprisingly, Massie didn't feel ready for any of them. And she wouldn't until . . .

a) . . . she was reunited with the Pretty Committee.

b) . . . she got at least ten ego-boosting compliments.

c) . . . she applied more peach gloss.

Massie gripped Claire's thin arm and pulled her close. "Who's where?" she asked again, this time through a fake smile, in case the boys were watching.

Wiggling out from Massie's tightening grip, Claire pointed at the massive oak in the center of the lawn. "The girls. They're under the tree."

A giddy flutter snaked through Massie's insides when she saw her best friends. The Pretty Committee hadn't been united for three whole months. And summering without them had left a lonely, gaping hole behind her abs that all the spicy tuna rolls in Japan couldn't fill. But seeing them now, standing bare leg to bare leg, comparing tans in their favorite meeting spot, renewed her hope. And made her feel 110 percent again. Together, they would stop this Briarwood virus from spreading. Then they would reboot and come out even stronger. Because that's what alphas do. And they were true alphas—whether anyone remembered it or not.

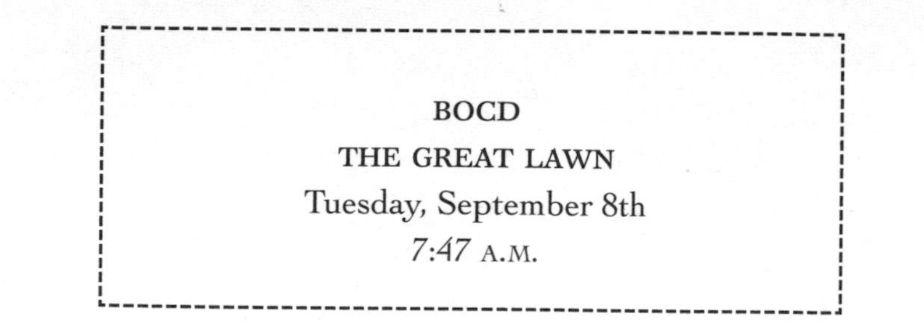

"Heyyyyy." Massie walk-waved as she hurried toward the oak.

"Heyyyyyyyyyyyyyyy!" the girls squealed back. They dropped their designer purses on the moist grass, ran to her with open arms, and collided in a forceful group hug, Massie blissfully at its center.

A blend of familiar fruity and exotic perfumes enveloped her, calming her even more. Alicia was still wearing Angel (spicy chocolate), Dylan was dabbling in Missoni (exotic amber notes), Kristen had stayed true to Juicy Couture (crushed leaves meets green apple), and Claire smelled like drugstore-bought vanilla-scented body oil. Or was it marshmallow? Either way, it smelled like cheap.

By the time they separated to scan each other's outfits, the smile on Massie's face was 100 percent toothy and 200 percent genuine. Maybe now the new kids would see how deeply she was adored. You couldn't slap a dollar amount on that kind of advertising.

"Let's sit." She linked arms with her BFFs and led them back to the oak with back-and-better-than-ever bounce.

"So, has anyone seen them yet?" Alicia asked in a hushed tone.

A heavy silence followed.

"Not even a distant sighting?" Claire snapped, obviously starving for some word on Cam Fisher.

Everyone shook their heads no.

Massie pressed her high-glossed lips together, fighting back the army of expletives marching up the back of her throat. Why was *everyone* so obsessed with boys these days? Wasn't she enough anymore? What had she done to deserve this? And who could she pay to make it all change? She thought of the light blue bag inside her purse and hoped to Gawd its contents would put her back on top—at least with the Pretty Committee.

"Soooo . . ." Dylan hand-fanned her pits once the girls ducked under the leafy shade of the tree. She pulled out the black hair stick that held her red hair in place. After three quick neck tosses and a rapid finger-comb, she put her hands on her hips and smiled for a camera that wasn't there. "You like?"

But the Pretty Committee was too busy propping their purses like beanbags to notice. Once they lowered themselves onto their designer leather cushions, she tried again.

"Um, thoughts please?" Dylan stroked her new hip-length, professionally straightened hair like a precious chinchilla. "Ay-sap!"

"Ehmagawd," they gasped in awe.

"I got it done at the spa in Hawaii."

"Love it!" Massie air-clapped.

The others followed.

Satisfied, Dylan smiled and joined their tight circle.

Two seventh-grade twin girls wearing burgundy OCD baseball caps and ill-fitting white denim J.Crew cuffed capris strolled by. Their heads were cocked as they clearly tried to figure out if the Pretty Committee's seats were actually *real* designer purses—and if they were, how they could be allowed to touch the wet grass.

"Um, excuse me," Massie called sweetly.

They stopped and stood close to each other, their skinny arms hooked for safety.

"Yeah," answered the prettier girl in the crisp light pink button-down.

"Do you work at the American Airlines ticket counter?"

They exchanged a puzzled glance.

"Then why are you checking our bags?"

The Pretty Committee exploded in laughter and sent the girls speed-walking for the school's nearest entrance. Massie watched her friends giggle-scan the campus for their ex-crushes. They were ah-bviously hoping the boys would spot them during a moment of extreme fun. But no such luck. The soccer boys were nowhere in sight.

After a final round of high fives, Alicia rubbed a French-manicured finger across Massie's indigo sparkle shirt. "I heart the shine. It's pure day-for-night boldness."

"More day than night, though, right?" Massie pressed, and then hated herself for leaking insecurity.

"Given." Alicia tapped a reassuring hand on Massie's charcoal gray satin shorts. Her tanned hands were covered in silver rings she must have picked up in Spain. "If anyone can pull off glitter on a Tuesday morning, you can."

"Thanks." Massie beamed, compliments stacking up like gold bangles. "Um, same with your open-toed ankle boots," she lied in an attempt to start the year off on a positive note. "Are they European?" she asked, knowing how Alicia's taste in footwear always nose-dived after a visit to her cousin Nina in Spain.

"*Sí.*" Alicia proudly straightened her legs under her gold knee-length peasant skirt and wiggled her feet. "They have the best shoes over there." She delighted in her Matador Red toenails as they poked through the otherwise normal sand-colored leather ankle boot.

"Saysyou," Dylan fake sneezed, sending a mass of straight red hair flying toward her beige gloss–covered lips. "Ugh." She plucked the strands off her glistening mouth. Without thinking, she wiped her sticky, tinted fingers on the sea green paisley sarong that was cross-tied around her neck and hung mid-thigh across her white leggings.

"Sorry. No one told me today's wardrobe theme was hotel gift shop." Alicia flipped her silky black hair.

"This is hardly from the spa." Dylan smoothed her sarong. "It's a prezzy from Ilana Slootskyia, my summer BFF."

"The tennis star?" Claire gushed.

"Tennis the Menace?" Kristen clutched the ivory shark tooth that dangled from a worn brown leather cord around her neck.

"Yup." Dylan French-twisted her hair and refastened it

with her black stick. "She was staying at the Kapalua. We hung out the entire time. I told you that in my e-mails."

"I thought you were joking." Kristen tugged one of her blond side-braids with excitement. "Now tell us everything about her. Don't leave one thing out. Start with her temper. Is it really as bad as they say it is? Did she really smash her boyfriend in the teeth with a tennis ball because he thanked the stadium soda girl when she handed him a Pepsi?"

Dylan rocked forward into a squat and grabbed her white quilted Chanel tote from under her butt. She unzipped it, pulled out a thick manila envelope, and handed it to Alicia.

"What's this?" Alicia held her chocolate brown knit cap in place as she leaned forward and grabbed the package. She started to open the seal, but Dylan swatted the envelope out of her hands. It landed beside her on the wet grass. "Why'd you do that?" She giggled.

"Um, I believe it's addressed to Mr. Rivera, nawt you."

"Why are you giving this to my dad?" The whites around Alicia's deep brown eyes shone, thanks to the smudges of dark green that she was now wearing inside her lower lids. Ah-bviously another Spanish trend she'd imported.

"Because he's a lawyer and that's a confidentiality agreement."

"Huh?" everyone asked at once.

"Ilana made me sign a confidentiality agreement so I wouldn't gossip about her."

"Not even for ten thousand gossip points?" Massie tried. "And a ring from ¡I!, the hawt-times-ten Spanish pop star?"

Alicia pulled a thick silver band off her left pinky and waved it in front of Dylan's emerald green cat eyes.

"And a week's worth of math homework?" Kristen offered.

"And, um . . ." Claire struggled for something to throw into the mix. "How about a Hello Kitty pencil?" She reached into her new white vinyl Mossimo for Target tote and pulled out a clear pencil case. It was stuffed with colorful new pencils that had all been sharpened to a fine point. "The erasers smell like watermelon."

"Um, sounds tempting." Dylan rolled her eyes. "But I can't. It's illegal. But I'll tell you this much." She paused while they leaned in closer.

Alicia licked her lips.

Massie took off her D&G glasses.

Claire tucked her hair behind her ears.

And Kristen air-clapped in anticipation.

"I'm starting a new diet today."

"*What?*" they giggle-shouted, and playfully whipped blades of grass at her professionally straightened hair.

"Who cares about your diet?" Alicia whined. "I want to hear about Ilana."

"That's why I need your dad to find a loophole in this ah-nnoying agreement. If he does, I'll open like an all-night diner."

"Done, done, and done." Alicia jammed the documents in her tan leather Marc Jacobs hobo. Massie was relieved to see that between her purse and her black RL cap-sleeved blouse, Alicia still had *some* taste left.

But someone had obviously gotten to Kristen. Her signature sporty-chic Puma style was out: Roxy Girl was in. She was wearing a pink-and-red striped romper with red platform Havaiana flip-flops, and carrying a canvas tote with a photo of a sun-soaked surfer careening down a sapphire-colored wave. Do-able in the O.C.? Maybe. But at OCD? Not a chance.

"Gawd, Kristen, you spent the summer tutoring. How did this happen?" Massie paused. "Unless that sac is vintage Chloé. Ehmagawd, it *is,* isn't it?"

"Nope. It's H&M. Isn't it cool?" She admired the photo.

A soft breeze rustled the leaves overhead.

"If I was stuck here all summer while you guys were traveling the world, I'd snap and go to H&M too," Dylan tried.

"Point." Alicia lifted her index finger, showing off a stack of thin silver braided rings.

"Snapping," Massie air-quoted, "is getting pierced at Spencer Gifts. Going full-on surfer girl is an identity crisis. And buying a cheap canvas bag at H&M is a major cry for help."

"I'm fine, okay?" Kristen assured them. "I hung out with the Baxters this summer and—"

"You mean that surf teacher who was going to run the wave pool at Briarwood?" asked Massie. "The one with that hawt son named Dude?"

"Dune." Kristen ripped out a chunk of grass and whipped it at her.

The girls cracked up, secretly giggle-searching the campus again.

Kristen smiled. "And Dune and I became friends and he gave me—"

"You don't have to make up stories so we think you had a fun summer." Alicia put her arm around Kristen's sunburned shoulders. "We love you no matter what."

"I'm nawt making up stories. I swear."

Rrrrrrrriiiinnnngggggg!

The bell sounded across the lawn and sent everyone running up the stone steps to the main entrance. The girls grunted as they took turns pulling each other up to stand.

"Wait, where's everyone going?" Massie looked up at them, just as a white puffy cloud blocked the sun, casting a chilly shadow across the frenzied campus.

Kristen pointed to the sprawling stone building. "The bell just—"

"Puh-lease." Massie motioned for them to sit back down beside her.

"What about the welcome-back breakfast?" Dylan pulled the stick out from her hair, letting it fall to her hips.

"What about your diet?" Alicia countered.

"What about coughing up the cash to pay for the rest of those boots?"

Massie giggled. She had missed their playful put-downs.

"What are we waiting for?" Claire asked. "What about getting to our table and—"

"We need to make an entrance, like we always do. If we file in with the masses, we'll be part of the audience. But if we go in late . . ."

". . . we'll steal the show." Alicia re-puffed her purse and sat. Dylan, Kristen, and Claire immediately followed.

"Ex-*actly*." Massie grinned like a proud teacher.

"Besides, I have something for you." She unzipped her bowler bag and pulled out five robin's egg blue Tiffany & Co. boxes. Each was tied with a white satin bow.

They gasped.

Suddenly, the campus was remarkably empty and silent. There was only the sound of a few chirping birds and the squeak of the school bus hiss-parking in the back lot. But Massie could have sworn she heard the thumping heartbeats of her friends as they stared excitedly at the little boxes on her lap. She silently counted to ten to heighten the drama—and then began to explain.

"From this moment awn, 'BFF' will have a new meaning."

They exchanged confused glances.

"Starting now, it will stand for 'Best Friends FIRST.'"

The Pretty Committee collectively nodded in agreement.

"This year is going to be all about *us*," Massie continued. "And only *us*. Boys. Are. *Out*."

Dylan held on to her smile, while Claire, Alicia, and Kristen shifted uncomfortably on their bags. Massie ignored their hesitation and forged ahead, knowing that the most convincing part of her speech was coming up.

"Boys make girls act like LBRs. Remember how lame we all acted last year?" She lifted her right brow and glared into each of their eyes. One by one they lowered their heads in shame. "I called Derrington *immature*. Meanwhile, I was the one kissing Skye Hamilton's butt so we could spy on Briarwood's sensitivity-training class. How immature was *that*?"

Everyone nodded with a mix of support and understanding.

It was the first time Massie had ever admitted she was wrong about anything. But doing so was necessary for her plan to succeed.

"Now, who would like to go next?"

The cloud passed. And sunshine returned, doling out its dwindling supply of summer warmth through the spaces between the leaves.

"Claire, how about you?"

"Huh?" She bit a cuticle on her thumbnail.

"How did a boy make you act like an LBR last year?"

She blushed. "I guess spying on Cam in sensitivity-training class and then getting the wrong idea and accusing him of cheating on me with a camp tramp named Nikki was pretty bad." She giggled nervously. "He hasn't returned a single one of my calls all summer."

"Are you ready to give up boys in the pursuit of fabulousness?"

Claire squinted up at the bright sky for a moment, then met Massie's gaze. "I guess?"

"You *guess*?"

"I mean, yeah. Yes. Yes, I am." Claire sat up tall.

Massie led the girls in a round of supportive applause,

then placed a light blue box on Claire's lap. Holding up a palm, she made it clear that the gift was not to be opened yet.

"Dylan?"

"I pretty much turned into Shrek." The redhead burst out laughing when she remembered how much she'd eaten—and burped—just to show Plovert and Kemp how "down-to-earth" she was.

"Are you ready to give up boys and focus on yourself and your friends?"

"Yup." Dylan beamed. "No guy is worth ten pounds. Even when it's two guys."

"Congratulations." Massie handed her a blue box.

"Kristen?"

"Easy." She smile-blushed. "I pretended to love romance novels and black nail polish because I thought Griffin Hastings would like me better."

"And what happened?" asked Massie, trying to suppress her victory smile.

"He dumped me." She giggle-shrugged. "Shocker, huh?"

The girls laughed with her.

"Are you ready to give up boys and focus on your friends?"

"Uh-huh." Kristen squeezed the shark tooth.

Massie held out her hand and wiggled her fingers.

"What?" asked Kristen.

"Isn't that from Dune?"

Kristen's mouth opened, but nothing came out.

"Well, he's a boy, isn't he?"

The soft breeze blew again, offering temporary relief to the heated moment.

"Isn't *he*?"

Everyone stared at Kristen expectantly, wondering what she would do next.

"Yeah," she finally said. "But the necklace is from his sister Ripple."

"I thought you said it was from Dune." Alicia's chocolate brown eyes narrowed.

"You were right." Kristen lowered her eyes and plucked a loose red thread from the bottom of her romper. "I lied so it would sound like I had a fun summer. Ripple made it for me. I'm over boys. I promise."

"Knew it!" Alicia slapped her own thigh.

Massie, determined to stay on track, decided to believe her . . . for now. Kristen accepted her box and sighed with relief once the attention shifted to Alicia.

"What?" She shrugged. "I didn't do anything embarrassing. Josh still has a crush on me and I still have a crush on him." Alicia beamed with pride. Her smile faded when Massie started tapping her nails on the last Tiffany box. "But I probably *will* do something stupid eventually, so I'll swear off boys too. Just to be safe."

Massie exhaled and grinned. She handed the box to Alicia, who snatched it up as if it were the last pair of sunglasses RL would ever make.

"I officially declare us the *New Pretty Committee*."

The girls applauded and began pulling at the ribbons on their boxes.

"Nawt yet!" Massie insisted. "You have to agree to the rules. As of this moment, we are on a boyfast. No flirting. No texting. No nothing. Boys are over."

Everyone gasped and exchanged side-glances.

"From now on we will focus on being fabulous and staying on top."

They applauded again and turned to their boxes.

"Nawt yet!" Massie snapped. "There's one more thing." She cleared her throat. "Failure to stay on the boyfast will lead to expulsion from the NPC."

The breeze stopped suddenly and the trees stood still.

"Ah-greed?"

No one spoke.

"Ah-greed?"

"Ah-greed," they muttered.

"Good. We'll have an official swearing-in ceremony after school in the bomb shelter."

"Can we open these now?" asked Alicia, her red toes squirming in her boots.

"Go ahead," Massie insisted, sounding more than pleased with herself.

"Ehmagawd," said the girls as they slipped on their new platinum charm bracelets. Five cursive initials—*M, A, C, K, D*—hung off each one, and a red heart with the letters *NPC* engraved inside swung alongside them. Massie's bracelet was the only one with a seventh charm—a royal purple crown covered with sparkling Swarovski crystals.

"Now, who's ready to go inside?" Massie jumped to her snakeskin-sandaled feet with renewed hope and energy.

The NPC quickly joined her and linked arms, their bracelets swinging and colliding, toasting their new union.

"Where's your old charm bracelet?' Claire asked as they swiftly made their way toward the building.

"It's gone." Massie beamed. "Just like the old Pretty Committee."

"I bet the new one will be much better," Dylan panted as she climbed the steps.

"It already is," Massie lied.

CURRENT STATE OF THE UNION

IN	**OUT**
NPC	PC
OCD	BOCD
BFF (Best Friends First)	BFF (Best Friends Forever)

BOCD
THE NEW GREEN CAFÉ
Tuesday, September 8th
8:06 A.M.

For the second time in less than an hour, Claire found herself hovering nervously outside the new Café.

"Principal Burns is introducing the new Briarwood dean," whispered Massie, her diamond-studded ear pressed against the frosted glass doors.

"What happened to the old one?" asked Dylan, finger-combing her red hair.

"Um, he probably got fired after his school drowned," Kristen suggested, oozing "duh!"

"Point." Alicia lifted a finger, sending her new charm bracelet sliding toward her elbow.

"We're getting close," Massie reported. "I say we enter right after the new dean introduces himself." Her amber eyes darted back and forth while she continued to eavesdrop. Suddenly she covered her glossy mouth to keep from laughing out loud. "I think she just said his name is Dean Don."

Everyone palm-snickered except Claire. How could she, when Cam Fisher, the beyond-cute boy who'd broken her heart, was on the other side of the bio-friendly walls?

All summer long, Claire had wondered if Cam found a new girlfriend at camp. Wondered if he missed her, even a little bit. Wondered if he'd try to get her back once he saw how tanned she was. And today, finally, all of her questions would be answered. Not that it mattered anymore, since she'd just stupidly agreed to a boyfast.

"Okay, he's at the mic." Massie turned to her girls. "Quickly. Everyone check the person to your left. Look for latte stains, smeared mascara, flyaway hairs, loose threads—anything that might say LBR."

Everyone turned left and speed-inspected their partner. Claire searched Alicia for signs of imperfection and came up with only one: impossibly pretty.

Massie searched Claire.

"Wipe those sweaty palms. Re-gloss. Pull the hair out from behind your ears. Roll back your shoulders. And for the love of Gawd, Kuh-laire, smile. We're about to make an entrance, nawt a condolence call."

Exhaling, Claire did what she was told, which wasn't easy, since her heart felt all twisted and tangled.

"Okay, the song we're walking to is 'Here I Come,' by Fergie," announced Massie.

"What part?" Asked Dylan.

"'*Get ready 'cause here I come. Get ready 'cause here I come. . . .*'"

Everyone nodded once.

"Good. I'll count you in." Massie gripped the handle. "Start silent-singing on six. I'll open the door on seven. We walk to the beat on eight. 'Kay?"

They nodded again.

Claire fought a rush of dizziness with a long deep breath. Fainting in the middle of the New Green Café while the New

Pretty Committee was making its entrance would be worse than awful.

"Here we go," Massie mouthed. "A-five, a-six, a-five, six, se-vuhn, eight."

They were *in*. Claire silently sang the lyrics while her feet stepped in time with the other girls'.

A thick mass of hot air enveloped her like a wool turtleneck in a heat wave. The New Green Café was at least ten degrees warmer than it had been when she'd snuck in to post the RESERVED sign.

Invisible clouds of floral perfumes, fruity hairsprays, powdery deodorants, and spicy colognes now eclipsed the earthy smell of fresh vegetables. And pressing down on that was a thick layer of hostility.

Every eyeball in the room suddenly glared at the Pretty Committee with *who-do-they-think-they-are?* resentment. Not one girl turned to her friends to envy-gush over their outfits! Not one boy slapped his buddy's arm because five super-hot girls were slinking by! The only sound in the room came from five NPC charm bracelets that clinked and clanged in time with their swinging arms.

Suddenly, Claire didn't feel like one of the cool kids who came late to the party because she had better things to do. She felt like an LBR who had been given the wrong address on purpose. Their magic had faded, which was exactly what Massie had said about her seventh-grade boots and handbags before donating them to the Briarwood fund-raiser auction.

Embarrassed and full of regret, Claire lost her place in the song. Suddenly, her left foot was going forward while everyone else's was going back.

If the other girls were panicking, they showed no signs. Their gazes were fixed on table eighteen like runway models staring off into some distant paradise that only beautiful people had the ability to see.

But not Claire. She *had* to look. Had to scan the overcrowded bamboo tables to see if Cam was there. Watching her. With his one blue eye and his one green one. Oozing Drakkar Noir. And wondering why on earth she'd agreed to this embarrassing late-entrance thing.

Layne Abeley, however, captured her attention first. She was seated at the head of number three, the only all-girl table in the entire New Green Café. Locationwise it was a dud: right next to the swinging steel kitchen doors, in the heart of the LBR section. Not that Layne seemed to care. She was waving her arms, crossing her narrow green eyes, and wiggling her brows, happily trying to get Claire's attention. Her mousy brown hair was knotted into two poofy buns, one above each ear, like Mickey Mouse. An assortment of pink and purple Hello Kitty pens jutted out from the left bun and three Chococat pencils from the right.

"Hey," giggle-mouthed Claire as she passed her only friend outside the NPC.

"Hey," Layne mouthed back with that warm, familiar smile that never failed to cheer Claire up. Even in times like these.

Just then, Principal Burns sighed impatiently into the

microphone. It sounded like Darth Vader with bad cell reception and was enough to make the NPC pick up their pace.

They quickly took their seats around their locally handcrafted table and studied its scuff-free mustard-colored surface. Each girl searched for her marking. Splatters from Massie's Purple Envy nail polish, hardened chunks of Dylan's chewed watermelon Bubblicious, Kristen's and David Beckham's initials written in orange Sharpie, the NO LBRS sticker Alicia had custom-ordered off the Internet, and Claire's fingerprints, added the day she was officially accepted into the Pretty Committee—all had vanished. Their memories stolen, destined to fade with their tans. Everything familiar was gone.

Principal Burns tucked the side of her chin-length wiry gray bob behind her ear, then fixed her black beady crow eyes on the NPC. The girls fidgeted with their purses and hems and hairstyles, until finally she cleared her throat and began explaining how the bathrooms and locker rooms would be divided.

Claire's rhinestone-covered Motorola vibrated, sending a rush of prickly heat from her heart straight to her feet. Was it Cam? Was he ready to forgive her for spying? But what if he was? Would talking to him violate the boyfast? She was too excited to think about such technicalities and lowered her phone under the table. Quickly, Claire thumb-flipped it open and checked her text messages.

Massie: What's wth evry 1? Not into us at all!?!?!

Alicia: Prob jealous.

Kristen: Doesn't feel like it.

Alicia: Point.

Dylan: They r boy cra-z.

Massie: Puh-thetic.

Massie: NPC rules.

Alicia: Point.

After several attempts to join in the conversation, Claire gave up. Her fingers had never been fast enough to keep up with them, and this exchange seemed to be moving at IM speeds. Instead, she read with one eye and scanned the New Café with the other. Determined to see through the crowd and spot . . .

Dylan: OMG there they r.

Kristen: ??????

Claire knew right away who "they" were. And her racing heart and sweaty palms confirmed it.

Dylan: The ex-ez. C Kemp Hurley? Majr summer-afro.

Alicia: OMG check out his T. Sayz "you've got male."

Kristen: Plovert's wearing the same 1.

Massie: Tak-eeee.

Pretending to care deeply about the boys' summer hair and perv shirts, Claire craned her neck to get a better look. They were sitting in the front, near Layne's table.

Hundreds of heads obstructed her view, but she was able to spot the back of Derrington's unmistakable shaggy dark blond hair. He kept turning to the side to whisper to some girl with long wavy blond hair. Claire strained to get a better look. The girl was sitting on some other boy's lap, but she was leaning forward to hear what Derrington had to say. Suddenly, her bare, narrow shoulders shook with laughter. She lowered her head to hide her giggles, giving Claire a better view of the boy whose lap she was sitting on. He had golden brown hair that covered most of his ears and was wearing a brown leather jacket and—OMG!

Dylan: Who's on his lap?

Claire wanted nothing more than to ask the same thing. But her hands were too shaky to type, and her stomach was threatening to spray jealousy-barf all over their new bamboo table.

Cam had *replaced* her. And judging from the girl's Hollywood hair, he'd traded up.

Massie: Looks like Ash Simpson.

Another quake of j-barf.

Alicia: Close. Olivia Ryan w/ an A.S. Nose job + x-tensions.
Kristen: 2nd nose job?
Alicia: 3rd.
Dylan: OMG! Josh Hotz sitting btwn Strawberry & Kori!

Alicia's cheeks turned bright red as she craned to verify her crush's location. Her brown eyes darkened with I'm-gonna-scratch-their-lips-off rage. If Claire hadn't known better, she'd have sworn Josh and Alicia were still hanging out. The possibility made her heart sting with envy. But then again, Alicia would never put her status in the NPC at risk by breaking the boyfast bond. Not even for a Josh Hartnett look-alike who loved Ralph Lauren and maid service. *Would she?*

Alicia: ? Is JH doing with those LBRs?
Dylan: Y r they allowed at the soccer table?
Massie: Y do u care?

She lifted her charm bracelet and shook it as a reminder. But the texts kept flying.

Kristen: S & K became BFF with Olivia at sum school. O's older bro Andy has a sk8 ramp. The boys rode it all summer and K, S, and O would watch. So ah-nnoying. Stalker much?
Alicia: Why didn't u tell us?
Kristen: NPC rules. Aren't we over them?
Massie: Yes! We! R!
Dylan: OMG! Is Derrington wearing jeans?

Massie shot out of her eco-seat, then quickly caught herself and sat. She had spent most of her Derrington days praying he'd get over his shorts obsession and get some cute jeans. And now that they were over, he had. It was *totally* unfair.

It was obvious from the alpha's flushed cheeks and hanging jaw that she was both hurt and angered by the sudden change—and probably wondering what, or *who*, inspired it. But she shrugged it off with an eye-roll and one final text.

Massie: Whatevs! Boyfast or bust!

Done, done, and done.

There was nothing left to say. And everyone knew it.

They'd made a promise and had the bracelets to prove it. And that promise was a good thing. After all, one look at Cam with Olivia, and Claire's stomach knotted up like an Auntie Anne's pretzel. It was unhealthy. *Boys* were unhealthy. It was time to cleanse.

The rest of the NPC must have thought the same thing, because they dropped their phones in their bags and fake-listened to Principal Burns while she thanked BMW for donating five silver "reverse vending machines" to their New Green Café.

". . . they will replace the smelly trash bins and give you a sleek place to deposit your empties." She cackled over the mic. "Once the machine is full, it will crush your recyclables and a lovely young British woman's voice, which I believe belongs to Keira Knightley, will announce how many UCBs the machine collected."

Everyone cheered like they knew what UCBs were and why it was so important for a machine to collect them. Or was it the stacks of pancakes being hand-delivered to everyone's tables by the teachers that excited them? Either way, Olivia Ryan's *look-at-me-and-Cam* "whoooooo" was unmistakable.

It was hard for Claire to imagine the skinny airhead feeling passionate about UCBs or breakfast, so she snuck another peek at the soccer table.

Cam was chewing and laughing with what had to be a mouthful of pancake. Then, in what looked like a flirty revenge plot, he grabbed a palmful of organic whipped cream and smeared it all over Olivia's glowing cheeks. Everyone seated at the soccer table cracked up and joined in. It wasn't long before the entire school was looking on with envy as BOCD's hottest boys marked their new love interests with the day's farm-fresh selection.

A faint jingle woke Claire out of her trance. She turned to find Massie and the rest of the NPC waving their bracelets around her ears. The clanging charms served as a reminder (or was it a warning?) of their new pact. She smiled appreciatively.

"Thanks," she managed, suddenly realizing it would take way more than platinum jewelry from Tiffany & Co. to help her get over the past. Way more.

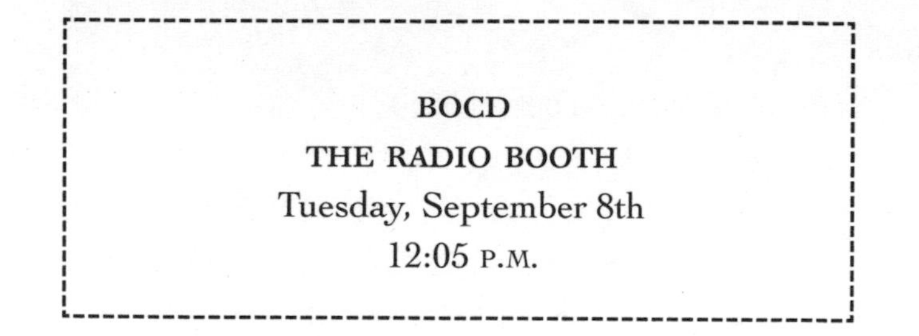

BOCD

THE RADIO BOOTH

Tuesday, September 8th

12:05 P.M.

"Oh five. Oh five. Oh five," Alicia mumbled while entering the code that unlocked the heavy steel door of the radio booth at the LBR end of the hall. The combination was the birthday of Principal Burns's fat orange tabby, Carrots—and a sworn secret, shared only with Alicia, the school's trusted anchorwoman.

Shockingly, she had been able to keep the combo to herself for almost a year now, but only because it had to do with her dream of becoming a TV journalist. Otherwise she would have spread it across BOCD faster than the story of Pee-Pee Perri Dorfman and her soggy sleeping bag.

The door made a kissing noise when it clicked open, and Alicia hurried inside. She craved the booth's soundproof walls and dim lights with the same intensity that she craved TSE's cashmere cowl-necks in February. Both made her feel warm and protected from the outside world—a world that was constantly telling her how to act, who to hang out with, and what boots to wear. And now, when to boyfast.

Alicia searched her black Balenciaga motorcycle bag for her ice blue bottle of Angel perfume. After a few sprays, the stale airplane smell was gone and the booth felt like home again.

"Nice boots!" She heard a boy cough.

She quickly covered her chest.

"I said *boots*, not—"

"Ehmagawd, what are *you* doing here?" Alicia blushed at the sound of her own excitement. "How did you get in?"

She turned up the dimmer switch on the gray-carpeted wall, adding some, but not much, light to the spray tanning booth–size room.

"Surprise!" Leaning against the knob-filled soundboard, grinning back at her, was Josh Hotz, her olive-skinned crush with the thick black maybe-he's-born-with-them lashes and red licorice–colored lips. He was wearing the most ah-dorable navy-and-white striped Polo rugby and RL's machine-torn Vesey jeans. A dark blue New York Yankees cap shaded his face. But Alicia could still see the cute white fangs on the sides of his mouth when he smiled.

She adjusted her brown knit cap and smoothed her gold ruffled Spanish skirt. If only they were famous. The genetically challenged could find inspiration in their beauty. . . . Computer geeks could design avatars in their likenesses. . . . They could model in Ralph Lauren's fall print campaign. . . .

Suddenly the charm bracelet around Alicia's wrist felt extra heavy.

After jiggling the silver doorknob to make sure it was locked, she jiggled it again. Then once more, just in case.

"What are you doing here?" She hurried toward him.

"You make the lunchtime announcements, right?"

Alicia grin-shrugged, as if her job as school reporter were no big deal, even though it totally was.

Josh lifted himself up to sit on the wood console. He swung his legs playfully, showing off a pair of lime green flip-flops with mini Polo logos stamped on the rubber beneath his feet. "Well, I wanted to say hey, so I stopped by. I gave the janitor a twenty to let me in."

Alicia blushed again, thinking of the three messages he had sent her—or rather, the three messages she'd ignored—since the welcome-back breakfast. But what was she supposed to do? Explain the boyfast? How could she? That was against boyfast rules. Besides, it was complicated. And kind of embarrassing. "Oops, sorry. My battery is dead."

Just then, her phone vibrated inside her bag. Once . . . twice . . . three times . . . four times . . . five times . . . Ugh! Did it always ring this much????

Alicia blushed for the third time. She opened her mouth, but nothing came out.

Josh lowered the brim on his cap, lifted his distressed brown leather messenger bag, and hooked it over his slightly defined shoulder. A heap of brightly colored envelopes and glitter-covered cards spilled out.

"What are *those*?" Alicia felt her upper lip curl in disgust.

"Just a few welcome cards from the girls in our grade." Josh scooped up the pile and stuffed them back in his bag. "Oh, and a few from the seventh-graders too, I guess."

Judging from the heap of girly stationery, it might as well have been Valentine's Day, and Josh the only boy in town.

Alicia's heart was thumping, her ears were ringing, and her forehead was starting to dampen. Massie was right!

The boys *were* the new alphas. The Pretty Committee was out.

And that made *her* out.

She fanned her face, then sniffed her Angel-scented wrists to keep from passing out. How could she possibly look Josh in the eye knowing she had expired like fat-free yogurt? Faded like tan lines? Dried up like year-old mascara? Who would hire her to be a TV journalist now? Anchorwomen were smart celebrities. And her celebrity status was waning. At this point she could be a career blogger at best.

"Well, I'll see you around," Josh mumbled, reaching for the door like someone hoping to be stopped.

Alicia knew she had to do something. For her love life. Her social life. And her career.

The red digital clock said 12:11:36. Which meant she had exactly three minutes and twenty-four . . . twenty-three . . . twenty-two . . . twenty-one . . . seconds before her broadcast to make things right.

"Wait!" She turned all the switches and pressed every button she could find. Suddenly staticky white noise filled the booth. Between that and the soundproof walls, no one would hear what she was about to say.

Josh dropped his bag and covered his ears. She motioned for him to come closer. He did, trying his hardest to stay mad. But, like most boys, he was powerless in the presence of Alicia's exotic beauty.

"ListenIknowyouliketogossipasmuchasIdobutwhati'm abouttotellyouisclassified," she hurried. "'Kay?"

She held out her pinky.

"What's the finger for?" He smiled with amusement.

"You have to pinky-swear not to tell anyone."

"Fine." He rolled his eyes as if the soccer team were watching, then offered up his baby finger. "I swear."

They shook.

"Okay." Alicia inhaled deeply, silently cursing Massie for making her choose between her best friends and the most ah-dorable Ralph Lauren–wearing, gossip-loving hawttie she'd ever met.

"Here'sthedeal.ThePrettyCommitteeisnowtheNewPretty Committeebecuaseweareonaboyfast.Wearen'tallowedtohangout withboysanymorebecauseboysmakegirlsdostupidthingsand wedon'twanttoactstupidanymore.SoI'mnotallowedtotalkto youandifIdoI'llgetthrownoutoftheNPCforgood.Sowhatdo Ido?" Alicia searched Josh's eyes for a reaction, but they were shaded by his Yankees cap. "Say something!"

He snickered.

"You think I'm lame, don't you?" Alicia wished she could take it all back. "You think I should stand up for what I want and not agree to such a lame pact, don't you? You think I should—"

"I don't think anything." He lifted his bag again. Alicia fought the urge to throw herself on top of him and beg him not to walk out on her.

"I get it."

"You *do*?" she asked as the red digital numbers on the clock informed her she had forty-five seconds to wrap this up.

"Yeah." He stuffed his hands in his faded pockets and leaned against the console. "My friends told me I couldn't talk to anyone in the Pretty Committee because you were a bunch of stalkers and spies."

Alicia gasped. "Puh-lease! If you found out there was a hidden camera in one of our classrooms, wouldn't you watch it too?"

"Denied. Hypothetical. Leading the witness."

Alicia's stomach flipped. Her crush had just busted out courtroom drama lingo. Could he be any more perfect? She wished she had captured that moment on her iPhone so she could send it to her lawyer dad. If she had, he would have sent back his blessing in the form of a big blank check for the wedding.

"Sustained." She giggled. "So did you tell them you'd never talk to me again?"

"No. I said, too bad."

Alicia's heart beat out the Morse code for *I ah-dore him.* "Then what?"

"Nothing." Josh grinned, revealing his ah-dorable fang. "We're guys. It was over in two seconds."

"Well, it's so nawt like that for me."

"Here, maybe this will help." He lifted a pink New York Yankees cap out of his bag, removed her knit hat, and placed it on her head. It was such a cute gesture she didn't bother thinking about how goofy she must have looked in pink, or how the polyester blend might suffocate her hair shafts. The only thought running through her mind was, *Awwwwwww.*

"Think of Jeter when you wear it."

Alicia nodded like someone who knew who Jeter was.

"The guy is a real team player, but at the same time, he's not afraid to be the best. And to be the best, sometimes you have to quiet the voices in your head and do what's right for *you*." Shyly, he stuffed his hands back in his pockets. "My soccer coach told me that."

"Thanks." She giggled.

Josh Hotz made her feel better than a fresh blowout.

"Ehmagawd, I'm thirty seconds late! Hand me that yellow folder. The one on the top of the stack." Alicia quickly adjusted the knobs and dials and slipped on the big headphones.

Josh did what he was told, then leaned against the gray-carpeted wall and admired her while she got to work.

"Good morning, BOCD, and welcome to the first day of school. It's Tuesday, September eighth, and here are your daily announcements. Boys, your locker rooms are the ones with the big sign that says BOYS on the door. So no more barging into the girls' locker rooms and pretending it was an accident." Laughter erupted from the New Green Café. "The Tomahawks' soccer meeting will be held in room sub-C5 at four this afternoon, and this year's captain is Derek Harrington." Alicia felt a pang of sympathy for Massie, who had to sit there and listen to everyone applaud ex-Derrington. "And this year's captain for the Sirens is *Kristen Gregory*!" More applause. "Auditions for this year's Christmas show, *The Wizard of Claus*, will be held next Monday, so drama mamas, start practicing your audition songs. And for those of you sharing lockers, Principal Burns and Dean Don apologize for the inconvenience and promise it will be taken care of by tomorrow. This has been Alicia Rivera for BOCD news. I heart you."

Josh burst into a round of applause. "You're a natural."

Alicia grinned on the outside, and her heart leapt on the inside. Could he be any more ah-dorable? More than anything she wanted to share every detail of their secret rendezvous with the NPC. But the boyfast ruled *that* out. And if you couldn't brag about your crush to your friends, what was the point of having a crush?

Or friends?

"What's this?" Josh asked, leafing through a red folder he had plucked out of the plastic hanging file sorter on the wall.

"It's confidential." Alicia snatched it away before he could read another word. "It's got Principal Burns's announcements in it."

"Killer! Hand it over. Let's read it!"

"We can't." Alicia held it behind her back.

"Why not?" Josh tried to grab it. "Don't you want the gossip?"

Alicia giggled. His hunger for gossip was charming, and no doubt one of his best qualities. But they were in the *newsroom*. And here, gossip was known as a leak. And leaks were unethical in a big way.

"Come on, lemme take a peek. I swear I won't tell anyone." He wiggled his pinky in her face.

She giggled again. He was more irresistible than crème brûlée fro-yo.

"Fine." She turned her back. "But *I'll* read it."

"Yes!" Josh punched the perfume-soaked air. "What does it say?"

"Ehmagawd." She scanned the ivory OCD letterhead, her left brow arched in disbelief as the alarming news whizzed by. "*Due to the dangerously high capacity . . .*" and "*. . . quaint overflow building . . .*" and "*. . . located in the back parking lot . . .*"

"Ehmagawd." Alicia slowly lowered the paper. "This is more shocking than the skull 'n' crossbones clothing trend."

"*What?*" Josh reached for the announcement, but she whipped it away.

"Tomorrow at lunch they're gonna announce that everyone at tables one through ten will be transferred to an overflow facility until BO can find a way to make more space."

"What kind of *facility*?" Josh air-quoted "facility." *Awwwww. Luv him!*

"Doesn't say," she answered.

"But you're at table eighteen and we're at three." His warm brown eyes cooled with fear. "We'll be separated."

Alicia paused. Maybe that would be a good thing. If she didn't see Josh during the day, Massie would never find out they were talking. . . . But *not* seeing him every day would mean . . . well, not seeing him every day. And how depressing would *that* be?

"I have an idea." He pulled off his baseball hat and ran his hand through his thick dark hair.

Alicia had no idea what she adored more, his devious mind or the wavy hair that protected it.

"Tell me." She bobbed up and down on her Matador red toes.

"Swear on the Yankees you won't tell anyone." He held out his hat.

"The *Yankees*?" she screeched. "Who cares about—"

"Just swear!"

Alicia took off her cap and clinked it against his as if they were champagne flutes. "I swear," she said with a playful eye-roll.

"On what?"

She rolled her eyes again. "The *Yankees*."

"Good." Josh replaced his hat. "I'll e-mail the plan tonight."

"You mean you don't—"

"I will." He flicked the brim of her cap, then, without another word, opened the door and slipped out.

Alicia kept smiling at him even though he was gone.

Once the coast was clear, she jammed the pink hat to the bottom of her motorcycle bag until it was buried under more makeup than Paula Abdul. Then she turned off the lights and inhaled the darkness, willing her thumping heart to mellow. Something was making it beat furiously. But what?

The thrill of Josh?

Or the fear of Massie?

It was impossible to tell.

Love and terror felt exactly the same.

BOCD
HEALTH CLASS
Tuesday, September 8th
1:07 P.M.

A pamphlet called *The Complete Guide to Menstruation* whizzed by Claire's head. "Okay, health class with boys should be illegal."

"Fear not." Layne placed her hands on her hips like a brave superhero. "I'm protesting after school."

Giggles erupted from the back of the classroom, where a group of eight students were ransacking the shelves, searching for dirty reference books. Only five others were in their seats, but no one dared make eye contact. Simply being there, surrounded by posters of teens with sexually transmitted diseases, as well as ceramic uteruses, was awkward enough. Actually acknowledging one another heightened the embarrassment factor to an unmanageable degree.

Layne checked all three of the multicolored Swatch watches on her arm. "Where's our teacher? Day one and she's already late. We should get our money back."

"I hear ya," Claire said to the nude male and female mannequins by the blackboard that posed in a proud-to-be-naked sort of way.

Layne unhooked a turquoise mesh sack from the back of her wooden chair and fished around inside. "I wish Dempsey Solomon was back." She pulled out a tin of citrus sour Altoids and popped an orange candy in her mouth. "You want?"

Claire shook her head no. Tart anything reminded her of the ex-gifts ex-Cam used to give her. And her taste buds weren't over him yet.

"Dempsey got me into these." Layne shook the tin. "They're curiously sour."

"Where is he?"

"On an eco-adventure tour in Bali with his parents. He'll be back Friday. I can't wait. He's like the only cool guy I know."

"He *is*?" Claire asked, picturing the blond, green-eyed chubby gamer who worked the lighting board for the Young Actors' Program (YAP) at the community playhouse. "Isn't he the one who presses dollar bills in his textbooks to make them vending-machine ready?"

"Yeah." Layne beamed. "Isn't that so smart of him?"

"The one Massie calls—"

"Humpty Dempsey?" Layne rolled her eyes. "Yeah. But trust me, he's cool. You should go for him. It might take you mind off Ca—"

"I told you already, I'm on a boyfast." Claire blurted, grateful for the excuse.

"Your loss." Layne shrugged.

"Why don't *you* go for him?"

"Onstage romances are cursed. We decided to keep our relationship professional, except at birthday parties and dances. It's for the bes—"

"Ew!" yelped Krista Bassett, the pale blond who insisted

her green contacts were natural. "This one's called *Safe Sex* and it actually *shows* you how to put on a condom." She whipped it at the guys, who jumped back, as if touching the pamphlet, even by accident, made them condom users.

Krista and her thick headband–wearing friends squealed in delight.

Claire slid her desk an inch closer to Layne's, then muttered, "Massie was so right. Girls *do* act lame around boys." She sighed. "My year is going to be so much better now that I'm on a boyfast. In my last class, I didn't think about Cam for four whole minutes."

"Wow, impressive." Layne pulled a pink Hello Kitty pen out of her right hair puff and began drawing a daisy-shaped ring on her index finger.

"And I would have lasted to at least five if my French teacher hadn't mentioned the color *noir*."

Layne giggled. "What does the word for *black* have to do with anything?"

"Cam's cologne is Drakkar Noir."

"Ahhhh." Layne returned to her finger art. "I'm sure it will get easier."

Claire gripped her new charm bracelet. "Hope so."

"Check this out!" called a curly-haired guy in camo cargos and a navy hoodie. He held open the gray metal door of the Hygiene Closet.

Krista and the Hairbands raced over to see what was inside.

A burst of male laughter erupted as Cargo Pants paraded around the room on his tiptoes. "Do you like my new jewels?"

he asked in falsetto, while lovingly caressing the tampons that dangled from his ears. "Daddy brought them back from Pair-eeee."

"Ewwwwww." Krista and her crew covered their eyes in shame. "That's soooo gross!"

Layne stuffed the pen back in her hair puff. "They're acting like they've never seen a T before, even though Krista got her period at the sixth-grade carnival." She lowered her face into her hands and shook her head back and forth in an *I'm-so-over-this-place* sort of way. "The classrooms are overcrowded, locker rooms are being raided, and the quality of our education is going to suffer big-time."

Just then, a tiny travel-size sample of Secret deodorant flew across the room and nailed the naked female mannequin's left boob. Everyone cracked up.

"Take your seats please!" shouted a big-breasted pregnant woman dressed in tight white Hudson jeans, a gold chain-link belt, and a white V-neck stretch T-shirt that strained to cover her many humps and bumps. If it hadn't been for the dark brown roots and the overprocessed strawberry-blond Shakira curls, she could have passed for a heaping dollop of Cool Whip.

"I'm Gina James." Her round butt bounced and shook as she hammered her name on the blackboard with a pink piece of chalk.

The boys raced for desks at the front of the room.

"But you can call me Gina."

"Va," snickered a boy in a green army cap.

"That's Jeeeena." She turned around and smile-blinded the first row with her bleached veneers. "*Not* Jy-nah."

The boys burst out laughing.

Layne and Claire exchanged an eye-roll.

"It's going to take a lot more to embarrass me than that." She leaned against the front of her desk and crossed her ankles. "And probably very little to embarrass you." She grinned. "So watch it, or I'll have you stand next to Adam and Eve and make you name their body parts."

Army Cap slid down the back of his seat.

"Since it's a mixed-gender class this year, I thought it might make sense to teach you what happens when a man and a woman—" She was interrupted by a round of embarrassed giggles.

"No, not *that*." Gina waved away the ridiculous thought. "I know you already know about *that*. I'm talking about what happens *next*."

Everyone was silent. For the second time that morning, Claire's mind was not on Cam. All she could think about was the brutally uncomfortable sex talk her parents had had with her, seconds after she'd downed her third slice of Baskin-Robbins mint chocolate-chip ice-cream cake on her ninth birthday. They cornered her at the picnic table once all the guests had left and asked her if she understood the dirty jokes her older cousin Debbie had been telling. She shook her head and stuffed handfuls of jelly beans in her mouth while they went into disgusting detail about what happens when two people love each other. Minutes after they were done, Claire puked green in her new sandbox and still, to this day, had no idea if it was the ice cream cake or her father saying "penis" that had made her so nauseated.

"*This* is what happens." Gina reached under her shirt and pulled out a freakishly real-looking nude baby doll.

Everyone gasped and exchanged shocked glances while the teacher hurried into the hall and returned with a playpen filled with crying toy babies. She gently placed hers inside the pen. She smoothed out her shirt, which clung to her now-flat Alba-abs. "Since I am assuming you all know how babies are made . . ."

A few of the boys exchanged high fives.

". . . I am going to spend this semester teaching you how to take care of them," she announced over the mounting hysterics coming from the playpen. "Which is no fun at all, trust me. Especially when your husband and au pair leave you with the twins so they can go diving in Fiji."

Gina twisted open her half-liter bottle of Poland Spring water and took a long, cleansing sip. "Lucky for you, these babies are synthetic. But other than that, they will look, act, sound, and *smell* like the real thing. They cry, go to the bathroom, sleep, and eat. They need to be held, changed, clothed, burped, and loved." She shook a baby bottle filled with crumpled-up pieces of paper. "Each doll has been implanted with a microchip that not only makes the baby act like a baby, it sends data to my computer, telling me how you are responding to its needs. We will spend each class learning how to care for your children. The good news is, there will be no tests. I will know how you're doing by logging onto my Mac."

A sigh of relief blew through the room.

"The bad news is you will have to care for this baby all semester."

Murmurs and moans came from every corner. But Claire welcomed the challenge. The project would definitely take her mind off—

The classroom door clicked open. *Think of the devil!*

Cam mouthed, "Sorry," to Gina and hurried to the back of the class. Olivia Ryan entered behind him; the ivory cashmere hood on her tight, sleeveless sweaterdress was pulled down over her head like it might make her invisible and keep her from getting in trouble. She grabbed the empty seat beside Cam.

Claire could sense Layne glaring at her with pity. And suddenly it felt like the entire class was watching her, waiting for her to start bawling. Which she easily could have.

The temptation to turn around made Claire's skin itch. She was desperate to study him. Study Olivia. Study them together. Desperate to know if the heat on the back of her neck meant he was eyeing her. Or maybe it simply meant she remembered how it felt when he did. But she wouldn't dare look. Massie would have been proud.

Still, the possibility of being watched by Cam at this very second was creepy. It made Claire feel vulnerable and exposed and pathetic. Like naked Eve. But worse. Like naked Eve if naked Adam left her, alone and bare at the front of the room, so he could go hang with another, prettier mannequin.

Claire gripped her charm bracelet, begging it to give her strength.

"Names?" Gina demanded once the latecomers were seated.

Everyone turned around but Claire.

"Cam Fisher."

His voice sounded different. Harder. Colder. Weighted with experiences she knew nothing about. More like a hotel, less like home.

"Annnnnnd?" Gina asked.

"Olivia Ryan." She giggled nervously.

"Great." Gina smiled. "Cam Fisher and Olivia Ryan, I expect to see you both here tomorrow morning at seven a.m. for detention."

Layne looked at Claire as if they had just won a major lawsuit. But Claire hardly saw Cam and Olivia's punishment as a victory. All the detention meant was that her ex-crush and his new crush would be alone in a room covered with naked pictures and pamphlets on sex. Um, who was really getting punished here?

Gina click-clacked up and down the rows. "Each girl will reach inside this bottle and pick out a piece of paper. Her partner's name and baby's gender will be on that piece of paper. And both will be yours to deal with for the rest of the semester. No trading. Believe me, if I could have traded partners, I would've. But unfortunately, life doesn't work that way."

Gina stuck an Avent bottle in front of Krista's face. Trembling, Krista reached her silver-manicured fingers inside and pinched out a piece of paper. Slowly, she leaned back and opened it in front of her friend Mara, a stringy-haired brunette with a face full of freckles. They tittered with delight.

"As soon as you pick a name, please join your partner and select the appropriate baby from the playpen. From that moment on, you will sit together."

Hands reached into the bottle, unions were formed, and babies were selected. One minute Claire prayed she'd pick Cam, and the next she prayed she wouldn't. The thought of him raising a baby with someone else made her feel like puking green all over again. But raising a baby together would be too difficult. What if they rekindled their love? What if they didn't? Either way, it would be impossible to get over him if they had to spend every second together. And that would jeopardize her place in the NPC, not to mention her sleep, her grades, and her entire digestive system. The best she could hope for was that Layne picked him. That way Claire could rest knowing he wasn't falling for his partner. Nothing against Layne, but if Dempsey Solomon was her idea of cool, she'd never like Cam Fisher. He wasn't nearly *ew* enough.

"Yes!" Olivia blurted. "Whassup, my baby daddy?" The unmistakable slap of a high five forced Claire to turn.

Cam and Olivia were palm to palm, gushing like perfect valentines. They strolled to the front of the class and hovered over the playpen, in search of the perfect baby girl.

Layne slapped Claire's arm. "Don't stare."

"Next." Gina waved the bottle in front of Layne's face.

Claire stood, desperate for a secluded bathroom stall and a tube of waterproof mascara. "I have to get out of here."

"Not now!" Layne whisper-begged. "Don't you want to see who I get?"

Claire wiped her stinging eyes and sat while Layne fished out a name.

"Pete Ehrlich?" She searched the room until she spotted the only guy left in his seat. His dirty blond shoulder length hair was parted down the middle, framing the sides of his oily face like soiled motel curtains. Layne mimed barfing in her mouth and then flipped the paper. "What does 'T' mean?"

"Twins." Gina snickered. "G'luck with that."

"But—" Layne tried to protest, but Gina had already moved on to Claire.

Gina held out the bottle, her liquid brown eyes fixed on the back of the room, where Olivia and Cam were cracking each other up with baby-name suggestions.

"How about we call her the Pied Pooper?" Olivia suggested as she fanned the air.

Cam laughed, even though a silly joke like that was beneath him. At least it used to be.

Claire returned her attention to the bottle, which Gina was waving under her chin. "Um, Gina? It's empty."

"Huh?" The teacher's gaze remained fixed on Cam and Olivia.

"There aren't any names left."

"I know!" Layne called from halfway across the room. She was balancing two crying babies on her lap while Pete picked a patch of dry skin off his droopy lower lip. "She can help us. We need it."

"I'd rather you join those two in the back." Gina tilted her head toward Cam and Olivia, who were in the middle of jamming their crying daughter into Olivia's yellow Kate Spade tote. They twisted and turned the baby until her chin rested on the lip of the bag like a teacup Chihuahua's. "They need help staying focused. Go be the stepmom."

"But—"

"That's not *fair*!" Layne shouted. "We have twins."

"Don't you *ever* use the F-word in my classroom," Gina snapped. "As far as I'm concerned there's no such thing."

"Why don't I become a single mother?" Claire tried, desperate for a way out.

"Cute." Gina rubbed her ringless wedding finger. "Now go." She pointed to the back of the room. "I have a few announcements to make before the bell rings."

Claire's forehead began sweating; her mouth went dry and her vision blurred. The sound of her thumping heart beat out her steps like a metronome. *Leftright . . . leftright . . . leftright . . .*

Without its steady tempo guiding her forward, Claire's legs would have noodled, and she would have collapsed.

Cam and Olivia didn't even look up when she approached. They were too busy marveling at how cute their baby looked with her bald head poking out of the bag.

"Hey, I know!" Olivia beamed. "Why don't we call her Kate? After my tote."

"Hmmmm." Cam closed his green eye and his blue eye. "Kate, clean up your room. Kate, time for bed. Kate, turn off the video games," he ordered with a playful smile, then opened his eyes. "Works for me."

"Yippeeee!" Olivia offered her palm.

They high-fived again.

"Um, hey." Claire stuffed her hands in the pockets of her khaki cargos to keep them from shaking.

The happy couple looked up as if she had woken them from a beautiful dream.

"Um, Gina told me to join your family and be the stepmom or something."

"What?" Olivia swung her yellow bag back and forth like a wrecking ball, attempting to soothe the crying baby.

"I'm the stepmom."

Claire side-peeked at Cam, who was watching the swaying bag in horror.

"Lemme try." Claire reached for the baby and lifted her out of the canvas tote. "There you go. It's okay. See? Everything is going to be fine," Claire cooed, more to herself than the baby. Kate stopped crying.

"How'd you do that?" Olivia asked in a hushed tone.

Claire shrugged the way a modest person would. But on the inside she was dancing circles around Olivia chanting, *I'm a better mother than you. I'm a better mother than you. . . .*

And then Kate threw up a cottage cheese–like substance all over Claire's back-to-school blouse.

Cam and Olivia burst out laughing, finally giving Claire the perfect excuse to run to the bathroom and sob.

BOCD
THE BOMB SHELTER
Tuesday, September 8th
3:50 P.M.

It didn't matter one bit that Massie was older and wiser and in the eighth grade. The cold, dimly lit metal staircase that led down to BOCD's boiler room freaked her out as much as it had in the seventh grade. And the smell of wet cardboard made her head throb. But, like a true alpha, she smiled through her pain.

"Hurry up," she called to the NPC, who, fused together in a cluster that resembled a well-dressed granola chunk, took each step with extreme caution.

"What are you so 'fraid of?"

"Murderers," Claire chattered.

"Ghosts," Alicia whispered.

"BO." Dylan fanned her sweat-drenched underarms.

"Burns." Kristen pointed at the low black ceiling, reminding everyone that the principal's office was directly above them.

"Puh-lease." Massie waved away their concerns. "We snuck down here all the time last year."

"It seems scarier today." Alicia's searched their dank surroundings, her dark brown eyes glistening with fear.

"So do your boots." Dylan burst out laughing.

Everyone cracked up, even Alicia, who looked down at her exposed toes and giggled.

It was as if the Spain spell had finally worn off and she was back in fashion reality. Her return was a sign that filled Massie with hope. Maybe by tomorrow everything would be back to normal.

"How awesome will it be to have our own secret room on campus?" Massie tugged the rusty door marked CAUTION! DO NOT ENTER. "No boys, no LBRs, no teachers. Just us. Just the New Pretty Committee!" she shouted, knowing that the clanging and steaming cylinders would drown out their screams. "To the NPC!" Massie lifted her arm and shook her shiny bracelet.

"To the NPC!" they echoed back.

Propelled by renewed excitement, they fearlessly dashed toward the boiler room, clutched the wobbly thin black railing, and made their descent into the school's bomb shelter. Correction: *their* bomb shelter. The one that had been handed down to them by Skye Hamilton, last year's eighth-grade alpha. And the one that they would hand down to the next generation of exceptional girls when they graduated. That is, if there *were* any exceptional seventh-graders.

"We're here," Massie trilled, searching her Be & D silver-and-black bowler bag for the key. Everyone crowded around her, blocking her light. But it hardly mattered. She knew exactly where the keyhole was. She'd imagined this moment at least a billion times over the summer.

"Do you think those racks of designer clothes will still be here?" Kristen asked, bouncing in her red platform Havaianas. "And what about the Starbucks machine Skye left for us?"

"And all of her Hard Candy makeup?" Alicia finger-combed her thick black hair.

"Get me to that buttered-popcorn maker." Dylan licked her lips.

Everyone glared at her with various expressions of mock doubt.

"What? It's low-fat."

"Um, buttered popcorn is to low-fat as Kristen's shark-tooth necklace is to valuable," chided Alicia.

"Is to Alicia's boots are cool," responded Kristen.

"Is to Claire is happy," Dylan joked.

"Is to Dylan's straight hair is natural," Claire managed.

Everyone cracked up.

Massie stuck her key into the foreboding black door to the bomb shelter.

In no time they'd be pledging their allegiance to the *New* Pretty Committee and swapping decorating suggestions for their exclusive new lair. They'd spend hours gossiping. Days laughing hysterically over nicknames they'd create for the boys. And months concocting rumors about the LBRs. Carpenters would custom build closets to store their magazines, which they'd pore over every Monday. Outfits would be preordered on Tuesdays. Accessory trades would be ongoing. Anything was possible now that the NPC had a place all their own. And nothing filled Massie with more of a joyful buzz than that. Not fat-free lattes, not Glossip Girl deliveries—not even the new-car smell of a Marc Jacobs bag.

Massie turned the key. The door clicked open.

"We're in!" she announced.

The stale odor of sweat mixed with duct tape flooded their nostrils.

"Ew! What is that?" Alicia pinched her little ski-jump of a nose.

"Did we forget to clean out the coffee machine before the summer?" Kristen twirled one of her honey-blond braids.

Massie kicked the floor switch and the lights popped on.

"What hap-pened in here?" Kristen whimpered, while the rest of them stood at the doorway, jaws hanging open, breathing in mouthfuls of thick, sticky air.

A wall of slightly dented steely gray lockers had replaced the racks of designer clothing. The brass Starbucks machine was now a giant Poland Spring water dispenser. All of the Hard Candy makeup had been removed, and in its place was a stack of semi-crumpled sports magazines haphazardly jammed in the faux-wood IKEA shelves. Their pink fuzzy director's chairs were now aluminum benches that faced a white board covered in X's and O's and arrows. And their beloved disco ball was covered with five yellowing jockstraps.

"What *is* this?" Dylan wrapped her long red hair around her neck like a noose.

Everyone's eyes were on Massie, waiting for her to fix things. But for once, she had no idea how. This was too much to handle. Even for her.

Feeling faint, she wandered over to the benches just in case. Everyone shuffled lifelessly behind her.

"We should complain." Dylan straddle-sat on the aluminum slab.

"To who?" Kristen plunked down beside her. "We're not supposed to be in here, remember?"

"I bet my dad could find a way to sue." Alicia stood, massaging Massie's narrow shoulders.

Claire lingered at the white play board and traced her finger over one of the X's. She sighed, hemorrhaging hope.

Unable to offer a decent solution, Massie felt like her powers had been stripped away. Like Dorothy without her ruby red slippers. Paris Hilton without the paparazzi. Jessica Simpson with dark hair. All she could think about was switching schools. But her friends needed her. And what kind of leader would she be if she bailed?

Gripping the purple Swarovski crystal–covered crown on her charm bracelet, Massie recharged her alpha battery. Seconds later, she was on her feet, ready to take charge.

"I'm guessing Skye came back for all her stuff." Massie paced alongside the bench. "Which is fine with me. The clothes would be outdated by now anyway, and Starbucks is so seventh grade. I propose a Pinkberry fro-yo dispenser."

"I heart that!" Alicia jumped up and air-clapped. "That store is in *US Weekly* more than Lindsay."

"What about a hair salon station?" Dylan joined her. "We can get a big mirror and a chair with a foot pump. And Jakkob can stop by twice a week for blowouts and straightening sessions."

"I want a Puma sneaker vending machine," Kristen added.

"That takes gum wrappers instead of money," Claire chimed in.

Massie quickly jotted everything down on her iPhone. "I'll get Inez in here first thing tomorrow to disinfect."

"Joyce will help," offered Alicia. "It's her day off on Wednesdays, so she's available. She'd love it."

"You think?" Kristen asked in disbelief.

"Given. Why else would she pick *cleaning* for her career? Because she *hates* it?"

"Sounds puuurrrrfect." Massie beamed. "Brody from RL Home will be here with a notepad and a tape measure by lunchtime tomorrow."

"Yayyyy," they cheered.

Even Claire.

"Now, who's ready to pledge?" Massie stepped up on the bench and held out her wrist, shaking the bracelet so it chimed.

Alicia and Claire stepped up beside her, while Dylan and Kristen took the opposite bench.

"Everyone please join wrists." Massie held out her arms. Her best friends' initials glistened, even in the darkest of times. "Now close your eyes. And repeat after me."

"And repeat after me," Dylan burped.

Everyone cracked up.

Once they stopped, Massie began the pledge-poem she had spent all of geography and half of Spanish memorizing.

"From this moment awn," she began.

"From this moment awn," they all repeated.

Massie smiled with satisfaction and recited the rest of the poem, the New Pretty Committee echoing each line after her.

I pledge the following to you.
To rid my thoughts of boys
Done and done, they are through.

I'll focus on fashion
Study new trends in beauty
Strengthen my friendships
And tighten my booty.

You won't find me flirting
Or talking to guys
No texting, IMing
No batting my eyes.

I'm above that now
Been there done that
Time for the LBRs
To have their turn at bat

Let them wear tight clothes
And watch boring soccer (no offense, Kristen!)
Let them laugh at fart jokes
Let them be the stalkers!

It's BFF time
No boys, not ever.
Because BFF has a new meaning
And that's Boyfast Forever!

"You may open your eyes.," Massie purred with post-yoga calmness.

Alicia hopped off the bench, and the girls released their wrist-grips.

"We're nawt finished yet," snapped Massie.

"Oops, sorry." Alicia stepped up. "Go awn."

Massie held out her arms again, only this time she kept her eyes wide open.

"Fail the fast and fail the group. Fail the group and lose the bracelet. Lose the bracelet and lose your membership to the NPC."

"I am so ready for this!" Dylan air-clapped.

The others gasped.

"Does that mean we can't even *talk* to a boy?" Alicia sounded more afraid than curious.

Claire bit her thumbnail. Kristen squeezed the shark tooth around her neck.

"Put it this way: Treat the boys like you would treat your brother. You can ask for help or favors or money, but no flirting, crushing, texting, or dressing to impress. Done?"

"Done!" Dylan bellowed.

She was the only one.

"Done?" Massie asked a second time.

"Done," everyone replied.

"Good. Now, to start things off I figured we would—"

Massie was interrupted by the click of the door. They dropped each other's wrists and jumped off the benches.

"You were right, Mass," Kristen muttered. "We *are* done."

A rush of boys dressed in burgundy shorts and green shirts hurried in. Massie stiffened. *The soccer team?!*

Derrington in *her* bomb shelter was too much to process. Her palms flooded. Her pits prickled. And her personality was MIA. All she could do was stare at his muddy, grass-stained knees and hate herself for thinking the boy who'd dumped her at an eighth-grade party looked kinda cute.

"Look, it's more girls." Derrington ran a hand through his sweaty, dirty blond post–soccer practice hair. "Everywhere we go we have fans." He turned around and wiggled his butt.

"Ehmagawd, I should have known!" Alicia fanned her cheeks and paced in a tight circle. "I made the announcement at lunch!"

What announcement? Massie asked with crinkled brows.

"The Tomahawks soccer meeting will be held in room sub-C5 at four this afternoon," she air quoted. "I had no *idea* sub-C5 was—"

"We're like Beckham." Kemp Hurley high-fived the guys.

Massie twirled her purple hair streak tightly around her finger until the digit throbbed.

"So, what brings you here?" Derrington strutted over to the benches and glared at Massie. "Autographs?"

The guys snickered, forming a tight half-circle behind their star goalie.

"No." Massie struggled to keep her shaking knees from knocking. "We're not signing today. Sorry."

She exchanged a triumphant round of high fives with the NPC.

"Then why are you here?" Derrington pressed. "To apologize for spying and beg for our forgiveness?"

The Tomahawks laughed and moved in closer. Cam was the only one who didn't join them. Instead he camped out by the Poland Spring cooler, nervously filling, gulping, and refilling a tiny waxed-paper cup with water.

Massie dialed up her inner alpha and pleaded for something fabulous to say. But the call went straight to voice mail.

"Because we've talked about it. And we'll forgive you, *if*, and only if, you complete a few small tasks for us." Derrington folded his arms across his chest.

The boys high-fived again while the NPC eye-urged Massie to do something.

But what?

Her heart thumped like a little bunny whose feet were about to get torn off and made into key chains. The last time she'd felt this threatened had been at a crowded Southampton estate sale over the summer. She had grabbed a black satin vintage Chanel clutch that was ridiculously underpriced at eighty-five dollars and was immediately descended upon by a pack of Kelly Ripa look-alikes. As they got within grabbing distance, Massie froze. The grassy lawn spun, the sun intensified, and her Cookie Dough

Glossip Girl lip gloss evaporated. A tangle of spray-tanned arms reached out toward her. Luckily, the overpowering smell of freesia perfume woke her inner alpha. Sudden bolts of energy zapped through Massie's entire body and fortified her with the strength she needed to escape. Without a second thought, she dug into her Coach tote, grabbed a crumpled hundred-dollar bill, whipped it at the cashier, and sprinted for the Range Rover.

Now, desperate for another lifesaving bolt of energy, Massie unzipped her bowler bag and quickly spritzed the air with Chanel No. 19. She inhaled deeply. The green floral wood notes, jasmine, rose, iris, ylang-ylang, sandalwood, and mosses filled her every cell. She was back.

She took a step forward and glared into Derrington's light brown eyes.

"Do you have a nut allergy?"

"No, why?" He glanced at his teammates in confusion.

"Because your head is starting to swell."

The NPC burst into laughter and slapped each other with a hearty round of high fives.

Derrington stepped closer. "Um, do you have a towel?" he asked evenly.

"No, why?" She fake-yawned.

"Because you're all washed up." Derrington wiggled his butt and bowed for his whooping and hollering male audience.

Massie gripped her purple crown charm. "Are you a sweater set?"

"No, why?"

"Because you've just met your match."

"Yes!" squealed the NPC, who danced and spun and wiggled their booties in a *ha-take-that!* sort of way . . . until Derrington countered.

"Are you Will Ferrell?"

"No why?"

"Then don't make me laugh."

"Oh yeah? Well, are you a calendar?"

"No, why?"

"Because your days are numbered!"

And with that Massie grabbed the NPC and yanked them toward the exit. Slamming the black door behind them, she and the girls broke into hysterics. They ran and giggled and panted and laughed all the way up the steps, through the boiler room, and out the side of the building, burning off the leftover adrenaline that exploded in them like fireworks.

Collapsing on the grass under their favorite oak, Massie accepted their nonstop congratulations on a job well done. But she was unable to take comfort in their praise. Comfort would come once the battle was won. And it was just getting started.

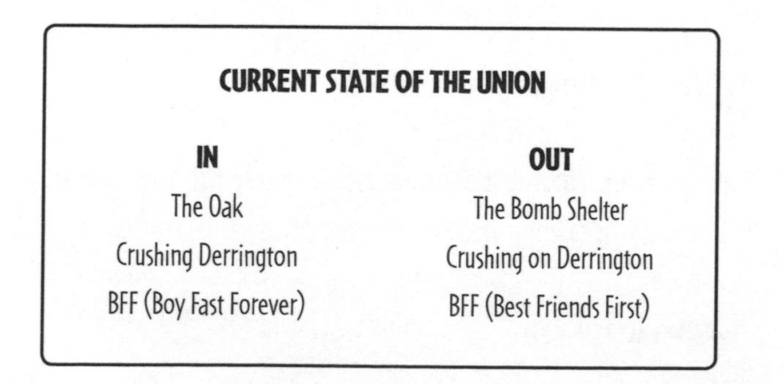

CURRENT STATE OF THE UNION

IN	OUT
The Oak	The Bomb Shelter
Crushing Derrington	Crushing on Derrington
BFF (Boy Fast Forever)	BFF (Best Friends First)

BOCD

THE SECOND-FLOOR BATHROOM

Wednesday, September 9th

12:01 P.M.

Someone in yellow Crocs burst into the girls' bathroom on the second floor. Alicia immediately lifted her waxed legs and pressed the heels of her kelly green canvas platform sandals against the beige metal door of her stall.

She had gone over the plan with Josh the night before on IM but was still nervous and needed one final round of reassuring texts before putting his plan into motion.

Before typing, Alicia triple-checked her iPhone to make sure the camera feature had been switched off. The only thing worse than Massie catching her stall-texting her crush on day two of their boyfast would be accidentally snapping a picture of herself on the toilet and sending it to Josh. Even though the seat cover and her white pleated tennis skirt were both down, it would be a complete digital disaster.

Alicia: R u sure this will work?

Her charm bracelet knocked against her phone as she typed.

Josh: Yup

Alicia: What if the NPC doesn't sit at #2?

Josh: They will cuz we'll beat them to #18.

Alicia: What if the guys don't wanna sit at #18?

Josh: They will because D wants to get back at M for not saying sorry when he gave her the chance. He knows this will freak her out.

Alicia lowered her iPhone, her mind racing.

Did Derrington honestly think he'd given Massie a "chance" to apologize? By what? Asking her to complete "a small series of tasks" while the entire soccer team laughed at her? Puh-lease! What did he expect her to say?

The sudden urge to call this whole thing off bubbled up inside Alicia like shaken Perrier. It would be easy. A few simple keystrokes, a light tap on the SEND icon, and this deceptive plan would be terminated. She could join her best friends at their usual table and not have to worry about getting brought up on betrayal charges. . . .

But then she'd have to end things with Josh . . . before they'd even started . . . and that would be—

Josh: U still there?

Alicia: Yeah.

Josh: Ready?

The lunch bell rang. Time for Alicia to make her announcements. Time to decide if she was going to go through with this. If it was worth the risk. If . . .

Josh: BTW, cute sandals. They match my shirt. Same green.

Alicia had her answer.

Four and a half minutes of awkward silence later, the toilet next to her finally flushed. After a quick click of the lock, Yellow Crocs squeaked toward the sink, pumped the soap, and ran the water for what seemed like days.

Alicia pressed her lips against the stall crack. "Ehmagawd, will you just leave already?" she snapped, unable to stay trapped in there for one more second.

"Huh?" asked the super-slim blond at the sink. She was vigorously scrubbing orange bronzer off the white lace blouse she never should have worn under a thin black cotton button-up jumper. The materials were mismatched, the textures fought each other, and the look was last year. Alicia wanted to tell her that she'd seen her outfit in *Madem*-EW-*selle*. But no one was there to laugh with her, so why bother?

"Um." The girl looked up. "Aren't you going to flush?"

"Huh?" Alicia turned around, wondering if she'd heard correctly.

"That's a little disgusting." She returned to her orange stain. "You were in there for, like, ever. And you didn't *flush*."

Alicia smiled again. Only this time it was full of fake. "What's your name?"

"Irika. With an *I*."

"Noted." Alicia hurried out.

She arrived at the radio booth at the same time as

Principal Burns, who was there to make her classified announcement.

"After you." The tall, thin, wrinkled woman with the wild gray bob and birdlike features reminded Alicia of a Dr. Seuss character. If she swapped her baggy tweed pantsuit for a red-and-white striped angora sweater and green leggings, she'd have her own Christmas special.

"Thanks." Alicia hurried inside the dark, stifling booth, dreading being trapped in there alone with the principal, who smelled like a mix of expired perfume and cat pee.

She reached for the folder with the day's announcements. After a quick scan, she put on her headphones and flicked the switches on the audio board.

"Good afternoon, BO, and welcome to your lunchtime update . . ."

Principal Burns held up a sign written in black Sharpie that said IT'S BOCD, NOT BO!!!!!!

"Sorry," mouthed Alicia, fighting a smile.

". . . starting with the lost and found. A brown row of hair extensions was found on the tennis courts this morning and is being held in Nurse Adele's office. . . . It's tee time for anyone interested in joining the girls' golf team. Sign up outside the gym. You must have three years of lessons and you must be a girl. Principal Burns is up next to make a few announcements, but before I turn the mic over to her, I would like to let everyone know that Irikawithan*I*doesnot flushthetoilet.TheNPCrules! This is Alicia Rivera for BOCD saying, I heart you."

Principal Burns opened her lipless mouth in horror, but Alicia tossed her the headphones and raced out the door before she could say anything.

The laughter in the New Café could be heard all the way down the hall, filling Alicia with pride. Thanks to her gutsy broadcast, Irika and all of her little seventh-grade boy-worshipping friends would know exactly who ruled BOCD. And that would earn her major loyalty points with Massie and the NPC—something Alicia figured she'd need very, very soon.

"As you all know, our beautiful institution has been a little crowded lately. . . ." Principal Burns's signature squawk crackled through the speakers.

The announcement was under way.

There was no time left for a pro/con list.

A choice needed to be made.

Would it be Massie or Josh?

Friendship or true love?

But all Alicia could focus on was how unbelievably unfair this whole thing was. *Why* should she have to choose? Why couldn't she have both? Why did Massie have to declare a boyfast? Why was Josh so ah-dorable? If only her father could sue the universe for being so cruel. But there was no time for long, drawn-out lawsuits. Alicia had arrived at the frosted glass gateway. And once opened, her heart would lead her wherever it truly wanted to go.

In three . . . two . . . one . . . and . . .

The doors burst open and Irika with an *I* suddenly bolted

out. Her overbronzed cheeks were now red and blotchy and salted with tears. "Thanks ah-lawt!" she sniffled, pushing past Alicia and racing to the bathroom.

Alicia rolled her eyes and resumed her countdown.

In three . . . two . . . one . . . and . . . With a single pump of the silver handle, she was in.

The earthy fragrance of ripe tomatoes . . . the dreamy gray light that seeped through the greenhouse-style roof . . . the heads that turned to see who dared enter late . . . the jam-packed tables . . . the sound of Principal Burns droning on about BO's dedication to solving the population problem . . . and Massie, frantically waving her glitter bangle–covered arms from table two—everything bombarded her at once.

All Alicia could do to stay on track was lower her head and snake her way to the back of the New Café, past the mini vegetable gardens, around the eco-friendly bamboo chairs, and beyond the silver BMW reverse vending machines.

Finally, she reached table eighteen.

Without looking up, Alicia plopped down in the empty chair. Kori and Strawberry were on her left, laughing at baby Kate, who was deposited in the middle of the table like one of the marzipan dove centerpieces at Cindy Starr's bat mitzvah party. Across the table, Olivia drew a skull tattoo on Cam's arm with yellow highlighter.

To her right were Derrington, Kemp, Cam, Plovert, and Josh.

Josh . . . !!

He winked, and Alicia lowered her dark brown eyes,

desperate for a place to hide, at least until her head stopped spinning. But that wasn't how they'd planned it. She was supposed to look surprised. Shocked, even. Something other than *ashamed*, or she'd never convince Massie that the whole thing was an accident.

But it was too late for theatrics. Her iPhone was buzzing.

Massie: What r u doing over there?

Alicia's mouth went dry as she tapped away at her screen. *Was she really doing this?*

Alicia: Last time i checked, this was our table. What r u doing over *there????*
Massie: Didn't u c me waving?

Alicia craned her head until she spotted Massie at the very front of the room by the steely kitchen doors.

"No!" she mouthed.

Even from that distance, Alicia could feel angry hate rays shooting out from Massie's amber eyes.

" . . . which is why I am pleased to announce that we have created a charming little overflow facility for some very lucky students," ech-hemed Principal Burns.

Alicia lifted her eyes and met Josh's. His relaxed grin seemed to say, "Don't worry, this is going to be great." Wanting to believe him, she blinked in agreement.

"So will everyone seated at tables one through ten please

gather your stuff and follow Ms. Dunkel and Mr. Hermann to your new home. Delicious snack boxes will be available to you for lunch, courtesy of Subway, so enjoy!"

The boys at table eighteen punched the sky and high-fived each other as if the Tomahawks had just scored the winning goal of the season. Olivia, Kori, and Strawberry snickered annoyingly into their palms. But Alicia remained seated and serious, unsure how to feel.

She could hear Massie and the rest of the NPC shouting, "Unfair!" "Illegal!" "Tricked!" "Duped!" and "Lawsuit!" over the building crescendo of voices in the New Green Café. But she didn't dare look their way. Alicia's head remained down, focused on the pleats in her skirt, until the entire front section of the cafeteria had been cleared out. And her best friends were gone.

BOCD
OVERFLOW TRAILERS
Wednesday, September 9th
12:34 P.M.

"Here we are," announced Ms. Dunkel when they reached the back lot. "Isn't it quaint?"

She blinked nervously, stuffed her chapped hands in the pockets of her ill-fitting brown poly-blend blazer, and forced her thin pale lips to smile. Ms. Dunkel's short, wiry curls covered her cone-shaped head like a helmet made of llama hair—something her bifocals should have pointed out before she left the house. "Trailers?!" Massie gasped, staring at the two long white metal rectangles. "Are you—"

"This is awesome!" beamed Layne as she rocked back and forth excitedly in her new black MBT shoes. The revolutionary curved sole was said to improve posture and help burn calories, but knowing Layne, she'd bought them because they were ugly. "We're like pioneers, starting a new society—"

"Puh-lease, we're more like the tortured cast of *Kid Nation,*" Massie interrupted. "This can't be right!" Her sparkly bangles clanged in protest. This was supposed to be her year to shine. To realize her full alpha potential. Not to get pushed aside by a group of egotistical boys and then sent to rot in a steel casket. This kind of thing happened to *other* people. Ugly people. Not her!

Just then, the gray sky started to mist, sending flecks of water that resembled beads of sweat onto the foreheads of all thirty-two overflow students (twenty-five girls, seven boys). But most of them didn't seem to mind. They just stood there in a happy-go-lucky cluster facing their new classroom, graciously accepting the yellow-and-green Subway snack boxes that the incredibly short Mr. Hermann was handing out.

Dylan quickly pulled a sea-blue-and-yellow Hawaiian-print sarong from her quilted Chanel bag and wrapped it around her long straight red hair. "If this rain makes me curl, I'm suing."

"I say we sue anyway," Massie grumbled as she covered her head with an emerald green Swarovski crystal–covered army cap.

"Maybe we can get our tuition money back." Kristen zipped her short-sleeved Roxy Hearts hoodie.

"At least it gets us away from the soccer boys," Claire whispered.

Massie expected Alicia to raise her finger and say, "Point," but then remembered she wasn't there. Which was a whole other issue.

"So . . ." Ms. Dunkel rubbed her chalky hands together. "Why don't we step inside and get started. Let's have the seventh-graders in the Mobile Learning Vehicle to the left with Mr. Hermann, and the eighth-graders can follow me into the MLV on the right."

Massie glanced behind her to make sure no one was

hiding in the bushes, waiting to snap her picture and post it on some loser Web site called FreakyOverflowPeople.com or something. But who was she kidding? There were no lush bushes to hide in. The only thing surrounding them was a fleet of economy-class cars that weren't worthy of the front lot. Oh, and a few dry brown weeds that even the rain refused to touch.

"Shall we?" Ms. Dunkel pivoted in her sensible fake-leather flats.

For the first time in her alpha life, Massie refused to lead. What was the rush? Instead she followed Claire, who teetered up the metal mesh steps in the wood platform Miu Miu sandals Massie had forced her to wear. But now that they were in trailers, Keds seemed more appropriate.

"Take a seat wherever you want," Ms. Dunkel said, as if that were some big privilege.

The LBRs raced to claim the rickety wood desks at the front of the room, while Massie and the NPC dropped their designer bags on four seats in the back corner by the wall. It was crucial that they stay as far away from the windows as possible. Even though they were scratched and marred with dust, people could still see inside if they really tried.

Dylan swiveled around and rested her arm on Massie's desk. "Smells like coffee breath in here."

Kristen stretched her feet out toward Dylan's desk and rested her green Puma slides in the loose metal book basket under her seat. "I bet it's infested with mold." She lifted her white sweatshirt over her nose. "And mold is the number-one cause of asthma."

Claire bit into the organic chocolate fudge cookie that had come with their Subway lunches. "It's so damp and chilly in here. We're gonna freeze in the winter."

Massie tossed her unopened snack box on Claire's desk. "Puh-lease. Are we in a coma?"

"No, why?" Claire tugged the short sleeves on her blue-and-green striped American Eagle polo, as if that might actually warm her up.

"Then what makes you think we're gonna take this lying down?"

The NPC cracked up.

"Attention back there." Ms. Dunkel pushed her bifocals on top of her wiry cone head as if they were Dior.

The girls rolled their eyes, then faced forward.

"I'm sure you've noticed by now, there are no lockers in here. So for now, while Principal Burns and Dean Don are problem solving, I encourage you to store your books and other personal belongings in wheelie suitcases."

Massie gasped. She loved her Louis, but *come awn*!

"The good news is all of our classes will take place in here so you won't have to drag them around all day." She pressed her hands together in thanks and glanced toward the heavens.

"That's *good* news?" Massie mumbled. "We're like inmates."

"Inmates," burped Dylan.

The NPC cracked up.

Claire raised her hand.

"Yes, um—"

"Claire. Claire Lyons."

"Yes, Claire." Ms. Dunkel squeezed her eyes shut, sealing the word into her cone brain.

"Does this mean all of the classes we were taking before are over?"

"That's right. I will be teaching you everything."

"Even *Health*?"

"Everything."

Claire sighed with relief.

"But fear not." Ms. Dunkel wheeled a portable blackboard away from the window, centering it for all to see. "I am fully qualified. Feel free to log on to my Web site and check my credentials. It's www . . ." She paused, then ran her fingers along the dusty wood slats below the board. "Hmmmm, no chalk. I'll be right back." She wiped her hands on her brown poly-blend skirt, leaving two white patches on the sides of her thighs.

"Poor Alicia," Massie sighed once she heard Ms. Dunkel's flats against the metal stairs—a delicate tap that somehow managed to shake the entire trailer. "She's missing all the fun." Pausing to see if anyone would take the bait, she spritzed her desk area with Chanel No. 19. But no one dared say a word. They were ah-bviously waiting for her reaction first. "So, do you think she did it on purpose?"

Dylan and Kristen exchanged side-glances.

"Do *you*?" Dylan finger-combed her hair.

Massie shrugged. "It *is* a little strange that she didn't try to come after us or switch into overflow."

The girls nodded in agreement as the trailer shook once again.

Ms. Dunkel returned, holding a fresh white stick of chalk above her head. "Mission accomplished," she panted, then turned to write her Web address on the board.

Massie scanned the classroom. "Who are all these new LBRs in our grade?" She whispered in Dylan's ear.

Dylan's shoulders shook with laughter. "They're not *new*. They were all in our grade last year."

"All of them?"

"Yes," Dylan whisper-giggled.

"I've never noticed them before in my life." Massie pulled a purple grape-scented pen from her turquoise Pucci pencil case and ripped a sheet of paper from her Claire Fontaine notebook. While Ms. Dunkel blathered on about her years of experience in the Midwest, Massie created nicknames for the LBRs in her class. Learning their real names was pointless.

She skipped over Layne and her two alt.com friends Meena and Heather, whom she had the displeasure of knowing thanks to Claire, and started with the girl behind them, fourth desk from the front, window side.

DESCRIPTION	NICKNAME
No upper lip, wide-set black eyes, gray sweat suit. Looks like a shark.	Great White
Overly rosy complexion covered in millions of tiny bumps	Braille Bait
Wild, frizzy, shoulder-length hair	Loofah
Super-dry hands, perma-curled into fists	Monkey Paws
Light fuzzy sideburns	Blond Lincoln
Carries books in plastic CVS bags	Bag Hag
Chunky goth girl who wears too much MAC makeup	Big MAC
Black-haired guy with cute-potential but has yellow teeth	Candy Corn
Very pale guy	Powder
Pink chubby guy	Putty
Super-tall thin guy with red hair. Always blushing	Twizzler

Ms. Dunkel left the trailer again, this time to get an eraser. Massie passed her list to Claire. Claire cracked up and passed it to Kristen, who cracked up and passed it to Dylan. Seconds later the NPC were laughing so hard they couldn't breathe

Until Layne climbed up on her desk, dressed in a red satin

blazer, a denim skort, red kneesocks, and her MBT sneakers. She lifted her fist in the air and shouted, "O-ver-flow! O-ver-flow! O-ver-flow!"

Heather, Meena, Great White, and Twizzler joined her solidarity chant, but the rest of the LBRs just watched in utter amusement.

"Come on everyone!" she shouted. "We have the chance to start something really great in here. Who's with me? O-ver-flow! O-ver-flow! O-ver-flow!"

Moments later almost everyone was standing on their desks, rocking the trailer with LBR spirit.

Massie grabbed her bag, "Let's get out of here before we catch something."

The NPC hurried to their feet.

"Where are you guys going?" asked Big Mac.

"Yeah, you can't leave," insisted Blond Lincoln. "We're in this together."

"You're, like, one of *us* now." Loofah beamed.

Those were the last words Massie heard before she blacked out.

BOCD
THE INDOOR POOL
Wednesday, September 9th
2:02 P.M.

Sitting on the moist aluminum bench, thigh-to-thigh with Strawberry, who was thigh-to-thigh with Kori, who was thigh-to-thigh with Olivia, who was thigh-to-thigh with Cam, who was thigh-to-thigh with Josh, was stressing Alicia out big-time. She tried taking a deep, relaxing breath but ended up with a nose full of chlorine fumes that rose off the pool like latte steam.

If she'd known the soccer boys were going to be in her swim class, she never would have gone through with Josh's plan. What if they made fun of her big boobs? What if her mascara ran? What if she got a water booger? What if—

Strawberry pinched the bell sleeve of Alicia's floaty white cover-up, rubbing the fresh linen between her thumb and index finger. "Is this caw-tton?" she whispered while Miss Kuznick took attendance.

"Spanish linen," Alicia explained, not knowing for sure if there was such a thing.

"I wish I'd worn something cute over my tankini." Strawberry poked the freckly roll of flesh that oozed from her red suit, where the *tank* met the *ini*. "I feel like a cherry tomato, and you look like a total movie star."

"Thanks." Alicia crossed her legs, allowing one black Prada

flip-flop to casually dangle from her toe cleavage. "I got it at the Lindo Hotel in the Costa del Sol. Their gift shop has the most ah-dorable stuff."

"Same place you got those awesome boots you wore the other day?"

Alicia gazed into Strawberry's emerald green eyes and nodded yes. Finally, *someone* appreciated her Euro-flair.

Kori leaned forward, her curved spine rippling under her hunter green one-piece. "I like your hair. It looks cool all slicked back like that."

Alicia ran a silver ring–clad hand over the hardening comb tracks on her head.

"I deep-conditioned before class."

"How smart is she?" Strawberry asked Kori.

"Majorly."

Alicia side-peeked at Josh, hoping he was listening. But he was too busy snicker-dropping a wet Band-Aid down the back of Derrington's gaping blue board shorts.

"Want some?" She held out a gold metallic tube of orange-scented Hydronectar Ultra Nourishing Oil Serum. "It will totally save your ends."

"Sure." Strawberry opened her palm, then finger-combed a dime-size dollop through her dark pink–dyed hair.

"Kori?" Alicia leaned forward, offering the goods.

"Thanks." Kori straightened up, sending her bony spine back into hiding.

Puuuuuuuuurpppp. Miss Kuznick's whistle echoed off the moist BriteSmile-white tile walls.

"Everyone in!" She tightened the pointless red visor that sat perched atop her short black-and-gray hair, then unzipped her white warm-up jacket and tossed it by the bench, revealing a sleek black one-piece that accentuated her Jessica Biel shoulders. "We're gonna warm up with ten minutes of power-treading."

Puuuuuuuuurpppp. Puuuuuuuuurpppp.

"Yeaaaaah," whooped Kemp, the notorious perv, as he dive-bombed into the pool. He quickly surfaced, wiped the mass of dark curly waves away from his close-set brown eyes, and shouted, "Come on, girls, show us what you've got!"

"Ew!" giggled Strawberry, Kori, and Olivia.

Alicia's cheeks burned. How was she going to take off her cover-up and get in the water without the soccer boys staring at her C-cups?

"Whoooooo!" shouted Chris Plovert during his front-flip entry. "Come on in!" He splashed the girls, who were trying to buy time, fiddling with their waterproof watches and over-tightening their ponytails.

Six more boys hurried in. Thankfully, Josh was not one of them. He sat patiently on his end of the bench, occasionally side-glancing at Alicia as if waiting to escort her.

Puuuuuuuuurpppp. Puuuuuuuuurpppp.

"Evv-rryone in!" Miss Kuznick shouted from the silver lifeguard tower.

Cam and Olivia, who were blowing up a pair of tiny pink water wings, held up their fingers to show the teacher that they would be in as soon as they could. Besides, it wasn't like Olivia had any reason to stall. Her lemon yellow Juicy one-piece popped against her buttery brown skin. And her legs had been freshly shaved and slicked with glitter-infused body oil. Her boobs were A's and her butt was an A+ . . . and she stood with the carefree confidence of someone who knew it.

Not that Alicia was worried that her body was worse than Olivia's. *Hardly!* It was that she knew it was better. More moisturized. More tanned. More cleavage. And *that* was the problem. She didn't *want* the attention, not when it came to her boobs. And especially not without Massie, who had always been there in the past to fire off a round of protective comebacks on her behalf.

Puuuuuuuuuurpppp. Puuuuuuuuuurpppp.

Three LBRs shed their nubby white towels and tiptoed to the concrete lip of the pool. "Ready?" asked the one in the purple racer-back Speedo.

"Ready," answered her friends as they pinched their noses and stepped in.

A swell of guy-cheers exploded from the water when they entered.

"DoIlookfat?" Strawberry whispered from the side of her mouth.

"No.DoI?" Kori asked.

"Impossible."

Puuuuuuuuuurpppp. Puuuuuuuuuurpppp.

They joined hands and stood. Strawberry held one out for Alicia, who politely refused it with a subtle headshake.

"One . . . two . . . three!" shouted Kori. And the two girls raced into the steamy pool.

Puuuuuuuuurpppp.

"No running!" shouted Miss Kuznick, who could barely be heard above the echoing screams of the treading pervs.

Aside from Cam and Olivia, who had been granted unofficial permission to dress baby Kate, Alicia and Josh were the only dry ones left. And there was no *way* Alicia was going to take off her cover-up while he was standing right in front of her. There was only one way out of this.

Puuuuuuuuurpppp.

She sat up straight and kicked off her black flip-flops.

Josh removed his blue New York Yankees cap.

She placed her conditioner on the floor.

He retied his burgundy-and-blue madras swim trunks.

She stood.

He stood.

She walked toward the pool's edge.

He followed.

"Take. It. Off!" shouted Kemp. "Take. It. Offfffffff!"

Alicia grinned like a girl with a plan.

Josh snicker-blushed, trapped somewhere between wanting to laugh with his friend and wanting to kill him for harassing his crush.

It was time.

"See *ya*!" Alicia shoved him, purposely using just enough force to jostle him, but not quite enough to knock him in.

"Hey!" He grabbed her wrists and forced her to the edge.

"Stop it!" she fake-screamed.

Puuuuuuuurpppp. Puuuuuuuurpppp. Puuuuuuuurpppp.

"No pushing!" Miss Kuznick yelled.

But it was too late. Josh threw Alicia into the pool. In her cover-up. *Oops* ☺!

Like a supermodel in a slow-motion underwater commercial for some new exotic perfume, white cotton parachuted around her while her silky, deep-conditioned hair fanned out in all directions. Once she was on the bottom, the cover-up settled against her body. Tiny victory bubbles escaped from the sides of her mouth, and she imagined Massie and the NPC gazing over the side of the pool, applauding her on a brilliantly executed plan.

The overhead muffled boom of Josh's cannonball entry shattered the fantasy but not the mood. And Alicia resurfaced beaming, feeling safe, protected, and humiliation-free. She slapped the heavy wet cover-up on the side of the pool, then joined her panting, treading classmates.

Cam finally slipped in the water, mindful not to splash baby Kate, whose arm was in Olivia's mouth as she slowly lowered herself into the water via the ladder.

Baby Kate burst into hysterics and squirmed to free herself. "Olivia, take her out of your mouth!" Cam shouted as he sidestroked his way to his rubber child's side.

Olivia released her canine grip and Kate fell into the water.

"You can't just drop her like that!" Cam shrieked.

"Why?" Olivia dismissed her overprotective baby daddy with an eye-roll. "She's wearing wings."

Alicia and Josh treaded and giggled, partly because of Olivia's cluelessness, but mostly because they were together.

"So spill it," Strawberry panted. "Why weren't you sitting with Massie during lunch today? Are you guys fighting?"

"Opposite of yes!" Alicia gasped at the mere implication and accidentally swallowed a gulp of chlorinated water. "It was a total mistake," she insisted, ignoring Josh's knowing underwater foot-nudge. "I thought she would be at eighteen and—"

"Is she mad at you?" Kori paddled into their circle. "You know, for ditching her?"

"I didn't ditch her, it was a—"

Puuuuuuuuurpppp.

Alicia was grateful for the whistle. The last thing she needed was to get bombarded with questions she herself had been struggling to answer. Besides, she didn't want to think about Massie right now. Because *now* she was playing underwater footsie with Josh. And his feet were rea-*lllly* soft.

WESTCHESTER, NY
WRAP STAR GOURMET
Wednesday, September 9th
3:53 P.M.

The NPC sat around a red horseshoe-shaped booth in back of the crowded 1950s-style diner, nervously tapping their manicured nails against the turquoise Formica tabletop. Claire, wishing she had nails to tap, picked at her mangled cuticles.

"So what's this emergency meeting all about?" Dylan finally asked, removing her chocolate brown leather blazer.

Massie spoon-swirled peach fro-yo around her canoe-shaped china dish.

"Yeah, just tell us." Kristen dumped a pile of salt onto the table, then carved a *K* in it with her finger.

"Let's give Alicia another minute." Massie checked the time on her iPhone. "If she's not here by three fifty-six, I'll start."

Dylan sipped her lemon water while eyeing a plate of cheese fries that were en route to a table of chunky seventh-graders. Kristen added a dash of pepper to her salt pile. Massie slapped her fro-yo with the back of her spoon. Claire gazed out the window.

A girl standing across the tree-lined street caught her attention. Like Alicia, she was wearing a white pleated tennis skirt, green platform sandals, and a white short-sleeved button-down with a cute little tie. But this girl was wearing a bright pink New York Yankees cap, and Alicia would never—

The girl took off the cap and jammed it in the bottom of her black leather bag. She waved goodbye to someone in the distance, looked both ways, then power-walked across the busy intersection. It *was* Alicia. The only person who refused to run, even while dodging SUVs during rush hour.

"Heyyyyy." She scurried over to their table and slid into the booth next to Claire. "Am I late?" She fanned her cheeks with the 1950s trivia place mat. "Wha'd I miss?"

Massie dropped her phone in the outside pocket of her shiny red metallic purse, refusing to meet her friend's chlorine-red eyes. "What's with the hat-hair?" she asked, somehow knowing, without lifting her head, that Alicia had a flat top.

Alicia quickly finger-combed.

"Were you wearing a *cap*?" Massie pushed her dish aside and finally made eye contact.

"What?" Alicia's tan shifted from brown to red. "Ew! No!"

"Bike helmet?" Kristen asked.

"No!"

"What about a yarmulke?" Dylan giggled, petting her long straight hair.

Claire shifted uncomfortably. She'd *seen* the New York Yankees cap. She *knew* Alicia was sneaking around with Josh. And that was totally unfair to the rest of them—but at the same time kind of understandable. If Cam still liked *her*, wouldn't she be doing the same thing? Or would she have had the strength to put her friends first? Not that it mattered, because Cam liked Olivia. And they had a baby. And . . . Claire reached for Massie's soupy, sugary fro-yo and began power-slurping, hoping the sudden cold would numb her brain.

"So it totally sucks that we got separated." Alicia pouted. "I was so freaked out when I looked up and saw that I was at the wrong table. I wanted to get over to you guys, but Dean Don was totally staring me down because I came in late. I'm totally gonna have my dad sue the school for keeping us apart and we'll use the money to buy new—"

"Why didn't you just ask if you could be with us?" Massie folded her arms firmly across her A-cups.

Three preppy eighth-grade boys strolled past their table on their way to the jukebox, jingling quarters and chugging Cokes from glass bottles. They slowed to check out the girls, who all lowered their heads to avoid breaking NPC protocol.

"Well, at first I thought maybe you'd *want* me to stay," Alicia tried. "You know, to have someone on the inside, keeping you up-to-date on all of the gossip. . . ."

Massie rolled her eyes.

"But, uh, then I decided it was a lame idea." Alicia absentmindedly glanced out the window, as if she was waiting for someone. "So I'm gonna try and switch tomorrow."

Claire slurped faster. Between Alicia's bad acting and Massie's doubting cross-table glare, she was seconds away from crawling under the table, rocking back and forth, and whisper-praying for everyone to *please* get along.

"Why were you sitting in the LBR section anyway?" Alicia asked, lifting ice cubes out of her lemon water with a fork.

"We were sitting in the LBR section because the Soccer Stalkers and our ex-crushes *stole our table*!"

Dylan leaned forward. "I swear, it was more embarrassing than getting checked for lice."

"Seriously." Kristen swept her salt pile on the floor. "At least the lice pickers have the decency to examine us in private. This was *totally* public. The whole New Green Café watched us walk to the LBR section."

"It *was* pretty bad," Claire added, trying to stay in the conversation.

Alicia's fake pout turned real. The corners of her mouth twitched. And the sparkle left her eyes. Was it guilt? Fear? Pity?

The jukebox boys strolled by on their way back to their stools at the counter as an old song about hound dogs blasted through the diner. This time they ignored the NPC, choosing instead to share their come-hither stares with a table of chocolate milkshake–sharing seventh-grade LBRs.

"So what's the overflow like?" Alicia twisted and turned her silver pinky ring. "Is it cool? I bet it must be fun being off on your own."

"Put it this way," Dylan chimed in. "Layne think it's supercool."

"Yeah, and I passed out because it was sooo cool," Massie snapped.

"You did? What happened? Was it a low blood sugar thing?" Alicia studied her friends, searching their faces for an explanation.

"More like a low point in my life thing," Massie offered.

"At least I don't have to be baby Kate's stepmom anymore." Claire tried to sound upbeat. She hoped Alicia would volunteer the latest on Cam and Olivia. But she didn't. So Claire tried again.

"So, how is the happy couple?"

Massie shook her charm bracelet in front of Claire's face.

"I meant, how are they doing as *parents*?"

"Who knows?" Alicia's eyes wandered toward the window again. "I've been keeping to myself the whole time. You know, cuz of the b-fast."

Massie's doubting glare lingered on Alicia for a few more uncomfortable seconds until she finally shook her head and refocused. "So, I called this emergency meeting today . . ."

Everyone leaned forward.

". . . to figure out how we can get rid of the boys and get our school back." She pulled out her new Palm T/X handheld and opened a fresh Word document. "Any suggestions?"

"Maybe my mom could do a telethon on her talk show to raise money for a new school," Dylan suggested. "We can have A-listers work the phones and beg America to call in with donations."

"Not bad." Massie nodded, tapping the suggestion into her PDA. "Anyone else?"

"Oh, I know!" Kristen raised her hand. "We could have a girls-versus-boys soccer match, and the losers would have to leave and—"

Massie lowered her Palm. "Do you awnestly think the Sirens could beat the Tomahawks?"

"Well, what if we make it so the losers get to stay and the winners have to leave?"

Everyone cracked up, even Kristen herself. But Alicia's smile quickly faded when the restaurant door opened.

Massie noticed Alicia's sudden shift. She turned around and came face-to-face with Derrington, Plovert, Kemp, Josh, Strawberry, and Kori. They all had damp hair and big cocky smiles.

"Ehmagawd, jeans again!" Massie whisper-blurted, and then blushed.

"Diesel," Dylan muttered from the corner of her glossed mouth. "They look cute."

"*Whatevs.*" Massie slapped Dylan's wrist. "Don't look."

The NPC lifted their lemon waters and sipped.

Claire quickly checked to see if Cam and Olivia were trailing behind the group, but there was no sign of them. Were they in his basement playing PGR4 on his Xbox? Doubling around the neighborhood on his black BMX bike? Sharing gummy worms on the swings at the elementary school? Claire gripped her NPC bracelet so hard, the point on the bottom of the heart charm dug into her palm and made it throb.

"What are *you* doing here?" Derrington asked, faking surprise. Kemp and Plovert stood by his side, snickering, while Josh and the Soccer Stalkers quickly filled the empty booth behind them. Alicia lowered her head even further, as if *that* would somehow prove to the NPC how uninterested she was in her new classmates. "I heard the diner just got an overflow section in the parking lot . . ."

Kemp and Plovert started laughing. Massie eye-urged the girls to ignore them and keep sipping.

". . . and I thought you'd feel more at home over there." He cracked up so hard, a gob of spit flew from his mouth and landed on the turquoise tabletop.

Massie lowered her glass with a slight slam and reached for a butter knife. She carefully transferred the spit bubble onto the shiny silver blade and held it out for Derrington and the boys to see. "Should we have this wrapped, or would you like it sent to your table?"

The NPC burst out laughing. So did Kemp and Plovert.

"No, I'll take it." Derrington swiped the knife from Massie and dashed to his table, his sagging jeans hinting at a pair of navy blue Jockeys.

"The boys have gawt to go," Massie whisper-insisted. She held out her arm and jiggled her bracelet over the center of the table, inviting the others to join her.

"Ah-greed!" They jiggled back.

But there was less force behind Alicia's jiggle. Claire had a feeling Massie noticed too. What she didn't notice was Kristen tugging on her mysterious shark-tooth necklace. And Claire peering out the window in search of Cam. Only Massie and Dylan were jiggling for real. That was when it all became alarmingly clear.

This boyfast, which was supposed to bring the NPC closer together, was starting to tear them apart.

BOCD
OVERFLOW TRAILERS
Thursday, September 10th
8:01 A.M.

Gale-force winds tore through campus, sending crushed diet-soda cans and crumpled bags of Baked Lays on a high-speed journey across the parking lot.

The overflowers huddled in front of the locked trailers, their cheeks getting whipped by their blowing hair as they clutched their wheelie suitcases and watched the sky change from mud brown to emerald green.

"How could they bolt the doors?" Kristen caught her red Roxy visor just before it blew off her head.

"How could they make us put our books in suitcases?" Claire sat on the edge of her brother's gray, hard-backed wheelie that was covered with Transformers stickers.

Dylan gathered her whirling red hair and wrestled it into a ponytail. "How could they put *us* with *them*?" She tilted her head toward the LBRs shivering beside them.

"How could they put *us* in *trailers*?" Massie kicked a can of Red Bull with her plaid vintage Burberry rain boots. They looked ah-dorable over her ivory-shimmer tights and hunter olive–colored Trina Turk tunic dress. It was a tragic shame to waste such a rain-chic ensemble on a musty trailer and a soon-to-be soaked pack of LBRs. But these days, alpha style was all she had going for her. And letting *that* go would be admitting total defeat.

"Sorry I'm late," Ms. Dunkel called cheerily from the other side of the parking lot as she speed-walked toward them, waving a cluttered key chain.

"I can't believe we have to stare at that outfit all day," Massie groaned, taking in their teacher's pleated black polyester slacks and scuffed, square-toed black ankle boots. The collar on her shiny beige trench coat was popped to block the wind.

"Look!" shouted Loofah, struggling to tame her haylike curls. "It's Winkie Porter, from the six o'clock news!" She pointed at the slender African-American woman taking long, leggy strides behind Ms. Dunkel.

The anchorwoman's hair was pulled tightly in a low chignon, accentuating her sharp cheekbones and signature periwinkle blue eyes. Her cream-colored pantsuit was an elegant mix of news-serious and fashion-forward. But her spiky gray Manolo Blahnik pumps were pure fabulous.

A bald, VH1 cap–wearing, pregnant-looking cameraman dressed in black denim ran backward, filming Winkie's determined gait, recording whatever it was she was saying into her handheld mic.

The LBRs squealed with delight and started snapping shots with their cell phones.

"Poor things." Massie pity-pouted. "They actually think they're seeing someone famous." She took a few steps back, purposely separating herself from the fandemonium.

"What's going on?" Claire lifted her digital Elph, but Massie slapped it out of her hand just as she was about to take a picture.

"At least *try* to be cool."

"Hey!" Claire hurried to retrieve her camera from the gray pavement. She shook it, listening for loose parts.

"Why do you think she's here?" Kristen quickly unbraided her side-braids, then re-braided them tighter.

Massie swiped an extra-thick layer of Blueberry Muffin–flavored Glossip Girl across her lips. "Maybe this whole trailer thing was a joke and we're on a hidden camera show," she said hopefully.

Dylan unzipped her black quilted Chanel raincoat and stuffed it in the outside pocket of her Louis Vuitton wheelie. She smoothed out her ruby red Alexander McQueen jumpsuit, undid her ponytail, then finger-guided her long straight hair so it cascaded over her left shoulder. "Either way, I'm ready."

Winkie positioned herself beside the eighth-grade trailer and continued speaking to the camera while everyone stopped talking so they could hear what she was saying.

". . . and this is what happens, folks, when a sister school reaches out to help her fallen brothers. It's a valuable lesson we could all learn a little something from." She smiled brightly as the cameraman stepped back, getting a wide shot of the two trailers.

"Isn't this exciting?" Ms. Dunkel squeaked with delight as she hurried by to unlock the doors.

Winkie strolled away from the trailer toward the NPC. "And now let's meet some of the selfless students at Briarwood–Octavian Country Day who were willing to give up their cushy classrooms and move into these overflow units until a solution is found."

Massie rushed forward, beating out Layne, Great White, and Powder.

"What about being *cool*?" Claire grumbled, but Massie didn't have time to explain the differences between star and stalker.

She grabbed the bottom of Winkie's mic and tilted it down toward her glossy mouth. "Hi, I'm Massie Block."

"Hi, May-seee." Winkie smiled.

Dylan, Kristen, and Claire giggled in the background.

"Actually it's Maaah-ssie, you know like sassy?"

A sudden clap of thunder made her jump.

"Of course." Winkie's smile flatlined. "So tell us—what's it like packing up your books and leaving your glamorous school behind for a couple of trailers?"

"This is a *special* group." Massie smoothed her blowing hair for the camera. "One that has no problem making sacrifices for the common good."

Just then, a bolt of lightning struck the back of the trailers. Everyone screamed.

"Those things are death traps!" shouted Monkey Paws, her hands clenched in tight fists as she ran in circles, screaming something about the dangers of metal in electrical storms.

"Get that!" Winkie shouted at her cameraman. He turned away from Massie before she could stop him and began rolling on Monkey Paws.

"Got it!" He swiveled back and repositioned his eye against the black rubber viewfinder.

Winkie licked her teeth clean of any possible lipstick smudges, then counted herself back in. "Going to tape in . . . three . . . two . . . one. . . . What's in there?" She pointed at Massie's enormous monogrammed Louis Vuitton steamer trunk.

"Just a few of my favorite textbooks." Massie folded her bare, goose bump–covered arms across her chest.

"Wow, you must have a lot of favorites." Winkie oversmiled. "Can we see some of them?"

"Um . . ." Massie turned around and glanced at her friends, who were now giggling into their palms.

Before she could dream up a good excuse, the cameraman crouched down on one knee, focusing on the trunk. Massie had no choice but to open it.

She popped the gold hinges and lifted the heavy lid. Packed inside were six vanilla-scented candles, two bottles of Purell, three soft white glare-free lightbulbs, five glass bottles of L'Occitane Cherry Blossom room spray, eight Nutz Over Chocolate Luna Bars, and four old denim skirts she'd asked Inez to sew into window treatments. All of which were necessary if she planned on surviving in the stinky trailers without passing out . . . or being seen. Not that Winkie needed to know any of that.

"Ehmagawd, my books!" she gasped. "I must have grabbed the wrong Louis when I left this morning."

The clouds turned black. Thunder roared. And suddenly, the sky dumped rain.

"My hair!" Dylan shouted, struggling to pull her Chanel raincoat out from the side pocket of her suitcase. "It's going to curl."

"Ehmagawd, my shirt is see-through!" Kristen threw her arms around Claire's back in a desperate attempt to keep her white training bra off the nightly news.

"Ew," Claire wiggle-giggled. "You're wet! Get offa me!"

"I have mascara in my eyes!" screamed Big Mac. "It burns!" She rubbed the sleeve of her soaked jean jacket across her face, smudging MAC makeup all over her cheeks until it looked like she'd run headfirst into a wet oil painting.

"Everyone inside!" Ms. Dunkel called from the open doorway. "Hurry!"

"No way!" screeched Monkey Paws. "That thing's gonna blow!"

"My books! They're gonna get soaked," screeched Candy Corn, his yellow teeth chattering as he dragged his wheelless suitcase under the trailer. Twizzler, Putty, Powder, Blond Lincoln, Braille Bait, Loofah, Great White, and Bag Hag immediately did the same.

Layne, Heather, and Meena, shrouded in matching green trash bags, joined hands, spun in a gleeful circle, and sang "Singing in the Rain."

"So, *these* are *my* best friends." Massie turned to yank Claire, Kristen, and Dylan in front of the camera, but they were gone.

Winkie pity-grinned, then shouted above the teeming rain,

"How about we take a look inside the *real* school and see how the others are coping."

The bald guy swiftly lowered his camera. Winkie flicked off her mic. Without a single goodbye or thank-you, they sprinted across the parking lot toward the regal stone building, as if their lives depended on it.

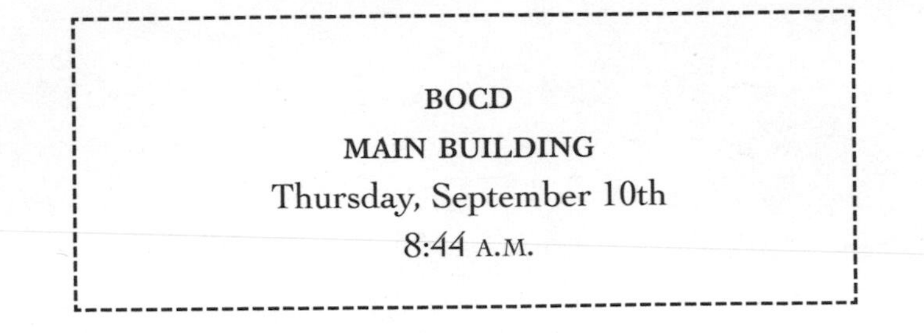

The second-period bell rang, liberating Alicia and Kori from a pointless biology lesson on frog parts. It was Alicia's only class without Josh and therefore a major waste of forty-five minutes. At least it gave her the chance to run to the first-floor bathroom to re-gloss and check the position of her pink NYY cap and—

"Ehmagawd." She grabbed Kori's lanky arm and dragged her down the hall, a sudden gesture that shocked the bony girl into dropping her notebooks.

"*What*? What's happening?" Kori quickly scooped up her clear binders to prevent them from getting stomped on by the mad rush of ballet flats and Pumas.

"That new teacher coming out of the bathroom looks exactly like the reporter on—"

"You watch *news*?" Kori stood, wiping dust off the knees of her cropped straight-leg Sevens. Her red-and-white gingham blouse and short stumpy pigtails made her look like a farmhand—the cute kind you see in fashion magazines, not the real-life ones that actually feed pigs.

"Of course I watch *news*." Alicia tugged her sleek black ponytail, which swung from the opening in the back of her pink cap and made her feel like a preppy RL model. "Mostly with the volume down, but still. If I'm going to be a famous reporter one day, I have to see how the anchors dress and style their hair and what makeup they use and—"

"Well, there *is* a cameraman with her, so maybe—"

"Ehmagawd, it's Winkie Porter!" Alicia whisper-shouted.

Thankfully, she'd ditched her blue-and-white striped Ella Moss T-dress when she heard the weather forecast and opted for baggy black Ralph Lauren Blue Label cargos, a wide silver belt, and a gray Vince ruffle tee. The colors said, "I'm serious about current events," while the playful cuts and luxe fabrics said, "And I'll deliver them in style."

Alicia decided she was at least a nine point three—it was time to make her move. She grabbed Kori's wrist and pulled her through the crowded halls, not caring how many designer bags she bashed into along the way.

The heady floral scent of Trésor perfume swirled around Alicia as she approached the sharply dressed and neatly coiffed reporter.

"Hi, I'm Alicia Rivera, BOCD's anchorwoman." She extended her right hand. "I love your shoes. Are they Manolos?"

Winkie smiled at her gray pumps. "Indeeeed they are." Then she gave Alicia's hand a firm shake. "Nice to meet you."

"Ech-hem." Kori fake-cleared her throat.

"I'm—" Winkie started.

"Oh, I totally know who you are," Alicia said, feeling her heart beat in her gums. "What are you doing here?"

Kori coughed.

"We're doing a piece on how OCD and Briarwood have joined together." She swiped a bloodred Shu Uemura lipstick across her mouth, then dabbed the excess on a silver Doublemint wrapper she had in the pocket of her cream-colored pantsuit.

"I'll take that." Kori held out her hand, obviously desperate to find her way into the conversation.

"Thank you," Winkie muttered, while gazing at the mad rush of students flirt-rushing to their next class. "We better get started before we lose everyone." She half-nodded at her cameraman, who immediately handed her a mic.

"Rolling."

"Great." Winkie conjured a wide smile. "Do you mind if I ask you a few questions?"

"Ehmagawd! Opposite of yes." Alicia smiled for the long dark lens.

Kori, having just returned from dumping the lipstick-covered gum wrapper in the trash, was freshly glossed. She stood shoulder-to-shoulder with Alicia as the passing students slowed to see what was going on.

"I am standing in the *dry* halls of BOCD, surrounded by the beautiful students who were lucky enough to hold on to their spots in the most prestigious learning institution on the East Coast. No trailers and rainstorms for them," Winkie announced. "And here to tell us why these kids made the cut is BO's very own anchorwoman, Ali—"

"Hi, I'm Alicia Rivera," She pulled the mic from Winkie's

hand and began strolling down the hall. The cameraman followed.

"I can't say for sure why some of us got to stay and others had to go. All I *do* know is that we really, really appreciate the sacrifice they made for us." A cluster of kids gathered behind her, bobbing and weaving, vying for their big moment on camera. "You have no idea how cramped and crowded it was in here before. It got so bad, the lady at the organic coffee station in the New Green Café actually had to stop giving people foam on their lattes because the lines were so long. It was brutal."

Suddenly, Winkie appeared by Alicia's side, gripping a second mic. "Do you think the overflowers feel discriminated against?"

"No," scoffed Alicia. "I heard from one of my sources that they think it's *super-cool*." She made air quotes around "super-cool" so everyone would know she was citing her source.

"Why do they like it so much?" Winkie asked. "Do you think they enjoy the feeling of helping others?"

"Whatevs. It's nawt like they did it to help anyone. They were in the wrong place at the wrong time," Alicia blurted, and then worried that she might have unintentionally blown some sort of press spin Massie had cooked up to make herself look like a hero.

"Some of those students seemed really happy," Winkie argued. "Three of them were literally wearing trash bags and singing in the rain."

This time, Alicia knew she couldn't possibly be referring to the NPC.

"I think *they* feel safe out there. No one can pick on them. It's better for everyone."

"So those people were sent away because they're less *popular*?" Winkie's expression was a mix of shock and elation—like someone who grabbed the wrong handbag by accident and found it full of cash. "Is *that* what you're saying?"

Just then, someone snuck up behind Alicia and tugged her ponytail.

She whipped around, ready to bark at whoever dared interrupt her during her interview, then saw her ah-dorable crush and giggled instead.

Cam and Olivia were beside him, trying desperately to quell Kate's latest tantrum.

"And who is *this*?" Winkie gushed over the baby.

"This is Kate." Olivia gripped the screaming baby behind the neck and waved her in front of the camera. "Isn't she cute? I named her after Kate Spade because she loves sleeping in my purse." The doll cried harder.

Winkie crinkled her penciled-on eyebrows in confusion.

"Where's that pacifier?" Cam searched the pockets of his Hurleys.

"How about this?" Olivia forced a pink lip gloss–stained straw into Kate's mouth and tried to coax her into sipping some Diet Coke.

The final bell rang.

Two couples hurried by, whisking their screaming babies off to health class.

"What's going *on* here?" Winkie gripped her abdomen.

"Oh," Alicia snickered, finally catching on. "The babies are fake. It's for health class. You know, to teach us responsibility."

"I see it's really working." Winkie rolled her eyes for the camera as Olivia yanked the straw from Kate's mouth and then tossed her at Cam, who managed to catch her just before she slammed into a Hello Kitty sticker–covered locker.

"Aren't they ah-dorable together?" Alicia asked, anxious to know whether Winkie approved of her new friends. Whether she thought they passed for alphas. Whether she thought Alicia was talented enough to be mistaken for their leader. "I totally approve. They are the best parents. I swear. And the cutest couple, don't you think?"

"They *are* attractive," Winkie gushed for the camera.

Alicia grinned with delight.

"But not as attractive as us." Josh threw his arm around Alicia's shoulders, then flicked the brim of her hat. He raced off to class before Alicia could swat him back.

"Well, you better get going," Winkie said as the hall emptied out.

"Yeah," Alicia sighed.

"I can stay," Kori offered.

"That's okay." Winkie half nodded to her cameraman, who then lowered the camera and wiped his beading forehead with the bottom of his black denim shirt. "We got what we need." She smirked.

Alicia scribbled her e-mail address on a sheet of vanilla-scented notebook paper and handed it to the anchorwoman.

"If you need a follow-up interview or even want a co-anchor or field correspondent, let me know."

"Will do." Winkie sounded impressed as she carefully folded the paper and slipped it in the side pocket of her pants. "And don't forget to watch tonight. Six o'clock." She slipped on her mirrored Dior wraparound glasses.

"I won't." Alicia offered her hand for one last shake, then caught her reflection in the lenses.

OMG!

Suddenly, instead of fantasizing about the countless agents and network executives who would beg her to drop out of school to become the youngest, prettiest anchor in television history, she broke out in a cold sweat.

She had been wearing Josh's NYY cap. On TV!

Her armpits, the backs of her knees, and her forehead were suddenly drenched in beads of liquid panic. It was a dead giveaway to anyone who'd known her for more than an hour that she was in severe crush mode. Why else would she wear something so athletic and pink on her *head*?

All Alicia could do was thank Gawd Winkie didn't work for *60 Minutes* or CNN. At least she was on the *local* news. And who watched *that*?

THE BLOCK ESTATE
GLU HEADQUARTERS/THE SPA
Thursday, September 10th
6:19 P.M.

Most nights, while her mother was cooking dinner and Todd was playing video games, Claire would curl up beside her dad on the tan corduroy couch and watch the six o'clock news. Even though they only spoke during commercials or those pointless stories about old people's birthdays, she associated the evening broadcasts with feelings of security and love.

But not tonight.

Tonight she was in the Blocks' spa, on a brown leather couch, sandwiched between Massie and Alicia, staring at a high-definition image of Winkie Porter, who was reporting on the rising tensions in the Middle East. And for the first time ever, Claire understood exactly what "rising tensions" felt like.

The only words Massie had uttered since school ended that day were, "Isaac, drop everyone at my house."

"Why?" Alicia had asked nervously, twisting and twirling her silver rings.

"Screening party." Massie leaned her head against the window of the silver Range Rover, as if a party were the last thing on her mind.

"For what?"

"We're on the evening news," Massie snapped. "Re-mem-ber?

Or are you people in Main Building too important to care about what goes on in overflow?"

Kristen twirled her shark-tooth necklace. Dylan checked her damp, frizzy hair for split ends. And Claire examined her swollen, red cuticles.

"I wasn't saying *that*. I was just—"

"Whatevs." Massie rested her head against the tan leather seat and closed her eyes.

After that, no one said another word. They followed Massie across the Block Estate's soaked lawn to the old horse shed–turned-spa, then dipped their cold, wet toes in the bubbling Jacuzzi while Inez raced to fill the room with ambience and snacks. Once the dutiful maid saw herself out, the NPC made themselves comfortable on the leather furniture and silently traded copies of *Us Weekly*, *OK!*, and *Teen Vogue* until 6 p.m.

But despite the soothing sound of water trickling from the limestone Zen fountain, the dimmed lights, the periodic blasts of lavender that misted from tiny holes in the ceiling, the crackling fire that cast a warm glow below the flat-screen TV, the strawberry-flavored iced tea, the humid earthy smell of passing rain that lingered after the storm, and Massie's ah-dorable black pug, Bean, who snored between them, Claire found it impossible to relax.

All she could think about was Cam and Olivia. Were they *really* a couple? What did they talk about? Why were they always laughing? Did he think Olivia was prettier than she was? Did he give her gummy worms and sours? Did he wear Drakkar Noir when he was with her? Did she smell it all the time, even when they weren't together? And did he miss Claire at all? Even a little bit? It took all of her strength not to come right out and beg Alicia for the gossip.

But the room was too silent for forbidden questions.

"How much longer till we're on?" Dylan stuck her pinky finger in the melted wax that pooled at the top of one of the vanilla candles, then shook it while it cooled.

"You know, it may not be good idea to watch this," Alicia offered. "Fact: A lot of celebrities don't watch themselves ever. They think they look bad, and it depresses them. That's why so many actors become directors. They're too embarrassed to go on camera again after they've seen themselves."

Kristen cackled. "That's not true!"

"It is!" Alicia lifted her palm as if swearing in a court of law.

"Shhhhhhh!" Massie slapped the thick brown armrest. "Here we go." She turned up the volume, then hugged her knees to her chest.

A shot of the darkening parking lot filled the screen. Soda cans and empty chip bags blew across the frame. The lens pulled back, revealing Winkie Porter—hair slicked, makeup matte, and BriteSmile smile gleaming. Her cream-colored slacks whipped against her toned calves, revealing the shiny points on her gray pumps. The scene looked like a storm update from the Midwest.

And then, Winkie, leaning against the dirty white trailer, began shouting above the whistling wind. . . .

"Winkie Porter here to bring you a heartwarming story of

sacrifice, generosity, and love. It all started when Briarwood Academy crumbled to the ground last May, leaving hundreds of students stranded without a school. That is, until Octavian Country Day opened its doors and hearts and took them in. But for many, that's when the real problems began."

The shot cut to the main building. The halls were crowded with students racing from one class to the other. But Alicia, who was strolling at a window-shopper's pace, seemed to have all the time in the world.

"It got so bad, the lady at the organic coffee station in the New Green Café stopped giving people foam on their lattes because the lines were so long."

Massie smacked the armrest on the leather couch. "Ehmagawd, you're *in* this?"

"I guess." Alicia peeled a layer of Matador Red polish off her thumbnail.

"What's up with that hat?" asked Kristen. "You hate sports."

"And pink," Dylan added suspiciously.

"And *sports*!" Kristen giggled.

"Where'd you get it?" Massie huffed. "And don't say Spain. Even *they* know better."

Alicia bit her bottom lip and shrugged.

Everyone turned back to the flat-screen.

"So what was the school's solution?" Winkie addressed the camera. "Trailers. Used trailers. In the parking lot." She paused to let that sink in with the home audience.

Kristen and Dylan cheered. But Claire was all too aware of

the mounting tension between Alicia and Massie to join them. An angry invisible force was spiraling around them, building and strengthening, like a tornado. And Claire was trapped in the middle.

Winkie continued. "One can't help but wonder how the faculty decided who stays and who goes. What criteria did they use to make their decision? And was that decision fair? Or was it a convenient way to rid the school of its special-needs students? Alicia Rivera, BOCD's anchorwoman, had some insights."

"Now no one will pick on them. It's better for everyone."

Dylan swiveled around in her leather club chair and faced the couch, practically spitting out her strawberry tea.

"What?" Massie jumped to her feet.

"No one will pick on us?" Dylan's cheeks turned red.

"You make us sound like LBRs!" Kristen clenched her fists.

"They twisted my words!" Alicia shouted at the screen, clearly too ashamed to make eye contact with anyone.

"Do you think the boys are watching this?" Claire couldn't help herself.

"Uh-oh." Alicia gripped her stomach and raced for the bathroom in the back of the spa. "Bad sushi!"

Winkie's expression on TV became serious. "Let's see if these trailers are, indeed, better for everyone."

The shot cut to the parking lot. A bolt of lightning struck behind one of the trailers and everyone screamed.

"Those things are death traps!" shouted Monkey Paws,

her hands clenched in tight fists as she ran in circles. "That thing's gonna blow!"

The sky turned black. A crash of thunder sounded, then sheets of blinding rain fell.

"My hair!" Dylan shouted.

"Ehmagawd, my shirt is see-through!" Kristen rushed behind Claire for cover.

"Ew, get offa me!" Claire wiggled away.

"I have mascara in my eyes!" screamed Big Mac. "It burns."

Candy Corn, Twizzler, Putty, Blond Lincoln, Braille Bait, Great White, and Bag Hag were dragging their heavy suitcases in a mad panic that seemed to have been sped up by the editor to look even more frantic than it was.

Then it cut to Massie. "These are my best friends." She smiled proudly. A shot of Layne, Meena, and Heather, dressed in their matching green trash bags and bellowing "Singing in the Rain," filled the screen.

"WHAT?" Massie screamed so loud Bean jumped off the couch and hid under a StairMaster. "I *so* did nawt mean *they* were my best friends. Ehmag . . ." She fell back onto the leather couch and buried her face in her shaking hands. ". . . aaaaaawwwd!

But Winkie wouldn't stop.

"Not exactly the best environment for kids with special needs. Not that the students in the main building seemed to care—"

"*Special needs!*" everyone shouted at once.

"For *them*, it was business as usual."

A shot of Cam and Olivia tending to baby Kate filled the screen.

"Aren't they ah-dorable?" Alicia gushed. "The cutest couple, don't you think?"

Claire slid to the edge of the couch. "Why would she *say* that?"

"They *are* attractive," Winkie had to agree.

The room spun. Claire's throat locked. Her stomach lurched.

"But not as attractive as us." Josh threw his arm around Alicia's shoulders, then flicked the brim of her pink cap, which just so happened to match his blue one.

The bell rang and everyone raced off to class. Winkie began strolling the empty halls.

"What started as an uplifting story of brotherly love ended up a tragic exposé of what can happen when a society strives for physical and mental perfection. We tend to dismiss those who are different, afraid that they may shine a light on our own *special needs* and force us to face the ugliness that lives inside each and every one of us. But carting them off to trailers is not the solution. In fact, it's the problem—a problem we cannot ignore. I'm Winkie Porter. Back to you in the studio, Greg."

"Different?" Massie clicked off the TV, then whipped the remote into the Jacuzzi. *"Special needs?"*

"Do I look that fat in real life?" screeched Dylan.

"Do surfers watch the news?" Kristen tugged her necklace.

"Do you think Cam and Olivia really are the *cutest couple*?" Claire couldn't help herself. It was bad enough that her ex–soul mate had moved on—and had a baby with a girl who was ten times prettier than she was. But did the entire *county* need to know about it? She had become the middle school version of Jennifer Aniston, without the good Pilates body.

"Oh, is it over?" Alicia asked innocently as she reentered the room. Too jittery to sit, she rested her hands on the back of the couch and shifted her weight from one foot to the other.

No one said a word.

"So?" She tried smiling. "Wha'd I miss?"

"You made us look like LBRs!" Massie hissed through gritted white teeth.

"No, I didn't!" Alicia pleaded. "They edited it to look that way. I swear! I would never—"

"Did they also edit it to look like you said Cam and Olivia were the cutest couple?" Claire shouted, shocking not only herself with her unusual show of anger, but the others as well.

Dylan, Kristen, and Massie held their bracelet-covered arms in the air, reminding Claire to be strong. The show of support was comforting, but not comforting enough. She felt humiliated and betrayed. By Cam, by Alicia, and even by Winkie Porter.

Massie stuffed her hands in the side pockets of her skinny Hudson jeans and ambled pointedly around to the back of the couch like a cowgirl. "And what was with that hat?"

"Um, it was a dare." Alicia took a few steps back. "Kori found it in the lost and found and—"

"Stop lying!" Massie shouted. Her voice cracked like she might actually cry.

Claire focused on the white sheepskin area rugs on the dark-stained floors. If Massie was going to tear up, she really didn't want to see it. Witnessing that degree of emotional vulnerability in her alpha was like catching her parents doing it. Deep down inside she knew it happened (ew!), but it was easier to pretend it didn't.

"I had a feeling you Alicia-ed your way into the main building to be with Josh. But I didn't want to believe it." Massie's voice was calm again, almost soothing.

"Wait! You don't understand!" Alicia ran her silver-ringed hand through her hair, the charms on her NPC bracelet bashing together.

"Actually, I do understand." Massie stepped closer until they were practically nose-to-nose behind the couch. She held out her palm.

"You don't!" Alicia's voice shook. "All my life, boys always liked me. They thought I was super-pretty or that my body was hawt or that I had good style. But for the first time ever, Josh likes me for me. And I like *him*. I've never liked a guy back, and now that I finally do, you make up this boyfast thing and—"

Massie opened her palm and wiggled her fingers.

Alicia looked at her open palm with tear-soaked eyes.

Massie wiggled her fingers again.

"Come awn!" Alicia stomped her foot. "It's so nawt fair! You all had a shot at love. It's not my fault you messed—"

She stopped herself just in time. "All I'm saying is that I finally had a chance to be happy, and I didn't want to choose between—"

"But you did," Massie said flatly. "You *did* choose. And you chose *him*. Now hand it over."

Alicia cried as she unhooked the bracelet from her wrist and slapped it into Massie's open hand.

The rest of the NPC lowered their gazes.

"Everyone please remove your *A* charms," Massie said flatly, "and throw them into the fire."

"You *guys* . . ." Alicia held out her arms and sobbed as she tried to appeal to Claire, Dylan, and Kristen for help.

But the girls did what they were told. One by one they pulled off their *A*'s and threw them into the angry orange flames.

Even Claire, who had once sympathized with Alicia, no longer did. Her comments about Cam and Olivia made it impossible.

"Now get out!"

"Come awn, you guys," she pleaded.

No one looked at her.

"Fine!" Alicia wiped her tears on the back of her hand and scooped up her black Balenciaga. "Dylan, you can forget about my dad finding a loophole in that confidentiality agreement." She jammed the pink baseball cap on her head and bolted toward the barn doors.

"I already did!" Dylan yelled after her.

Alicia paused, her hand on the doorknob, hoping for one last chance. "I can't believe you guys are doing this."

"You can't?" Massie sounded genuinely shocked. "Puh-lease! First you switch tables, then you make us look like LBRs on the news, and now you're wearing Josh's stupid baseball cap!" Massie shouted. "One, two, three strikes, YOU'RE OUT!"

Alicia threw open the doors and took off into the foggy, humid night.

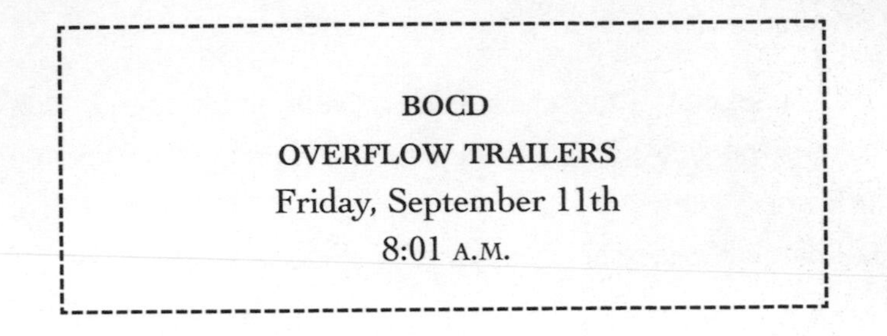

Sometime between last night's six o'clock news and Friday morning's first-period bell, a group of students from the main building t.p.'ed the outside of the eighth-grade trailer and plastered it with signs that said DON'T FEED THE CHALLENGED.

Inside, the overflow trailer was thick with hair-frizzing humidity and ripe with the smell of pencil erasers and sweaty bologna. The LBRs were seated, biology books cracked, and binders opened to last night's homework while they waited for Ms. Dunkel to arrive. The NPC, however, scurried about spraying L'Occitane Cherry Blossom room spray in every musty corner of the trailer while pressing vanilla-scented candles to their nostrils.

"You know, you should really check with everyone before you spray that stuff," Braille Bait mumbled, her bumpy face buried deep inside her peach-colored hoodie. "My skin is sensitive to perfumes and dyes."

"Well, my nose is sensitive to the smell of dead animal." Massie spritzed one last time before turning on the heel of her silver Tod's ballet flat and marching to the back of the room. "We have much bigger problems than your rosacea."

The *drip . . . drip . . . drip* sound of yesterday's rain seeping through the rusted roof backed her up.

Sensing an outburst, the NPC stopped fumigating at once. They lowered their nose-candles and joined Massie in the middle of the room.

"Bigger problems?" squeaked Braille Bait.

"Um, yeah! Didn't *any* of you watch the news last night?" Massie shouted in Braille Bait's face, causing her cheeks to gradate from fuchsia to deep burgundy. "Or see the outside of this trailer?"

The LBRs smile-nodded.

"Can you believe how much attention we're getting?" Great White beamed, the lids above her wide-set black eyes fluttering with joy.

"I know, it's soooo cool." Monkey Paws clapped.

"Your clips were sooo funny," snorted Loofah. "My whole family was dying when you were running around in circles screaming about the lightning."

"Mine too!" grinned Candy Corn, revealing a crooked row of slimy yellow teeth. "My au pair thinks you should get your own reality show."

"Thanks." Monkey Paws stood and bowed. "But the real stars were Layne, Meena, and Heather." She turned to the three girls, who were wearing matching homemade yellow GO WITH THE OVERFLOW T-shirts. "You looked so cute singing in the—"

"Ehmagawd, you people actually *liked* that news story?" Massie, overcome by another dizzying low blood sugar moment, wobbled like a seasick, stiletto-wearing Versace model out for a high-seas romp on Donatella's yacht. She bit into a Nutz Over Chocolate Luna Bar and willed the vertigo to pass. At some point Dylan, Kristen, and Claire started rubbing her back in gentle circles. Or were those angels? Airlifting her dead body to heaven?

Drip . . . drip . . . .drip . . .

Massie took a few more bites of her energy bar. And then, finally, the trailer stopped spinning. She raised her head slowly and found a room full of LBRs staring at her, their expressions a mix of mild concern and extreme fascination.

"You okay?" Kristen asked while fanning Massie's cheeks with her Roxy cowboy hat.

Drip . . . drip . . . drip . . .

"Do I *look* okay?" Dylan tugged her frizzy curls like a frustrated "before" in need of some vitamin-enriched conditioner. "That rain turned me into Carrot Top. And if someone doesn't stop that leaking roof, I'm gonna—"

"Nawt *you*," giggle-cackled Kristen. "I was talking to Massie."

Claire giggled into her palm.

"Yeah, I'm fine." Massie rubbed her burning eyeballs, which were the same hue as her quilted Marc Jacobs Banana hobo bag—bloodred. At least the bag added a burst of color to her outfit—a shimmering gray tunic-tank, which she wore over black leggings. Her eyes, on the other had, told the world she'd spent the night in agony, tossing and turning over the Alicia Incident.

Or maybe she should call it the Alicia Back-Stab Scandal.

Or the Alicia Chooses a Boy Over Her Friends Fiasco.

No matter what stupid name she invented, it all meant the same thing. She was losing control over her life. Her friends. Her enemies. Her beauty. And now her blood sugar. She felt like last year's boot-cut True Religion jeans . . . tucked away in the back of a closet and left to fade.

Drip . . . drip . . . drip . . .

Without another word, she raced to the back of the trailer and paced the row of wheelie suitcases parked against the empty wall. This leak *had* to stop.

She finger-tapped her chin, scrutinizing the luggage as if pondering which suitcase to roll down the red carpet at the Oscars. She passed over Kristen's red-and-white heart-covered Roxy, Claire's sticker-infested boy bag, Dylan's Louis Vuitton wheelie, and her own Louis Vuitton steamer trunk, knowing they weren't options. Neither was the sporty orange-and-black Tumi T3 Ducati, the cartoonish Tokidoki LeSportsac, or the three bubble-gum pink Hello Kittys (belonging to Layne, Meena, and Heather, of course). But the black scratched hard-shell Samsonite was perfect. She crouched down and unfastened the metal buckle. It popped open with ease as if to say, "Thanks for choosing me."

Quickly, she removed the Game Boy, iPod Nano, drink box of calcium-enriched soy milk, stack of graphic novels, swim goggles, and rubber nose-plugs—*ew!*—then dragged the open case across the dusty floor and positioned it three feet behind her desk, where the roof was *still* leaking from yesterday's storm.

"Hey, that's mine!" screeched the boy with the short light

hair and pale pink skin. "Where's all my stuff?" He blinked and then wiped his forehead with the bottom of his extra-long New York Knicks basketball jersey.

"Relax, Putty." Massie rolled her eyes. "Your nose plugs are perfectly safe back there. No one will touch them. I promise."

Kristen, Dylan, and Claire giggled from across the room.

The boy raced to the back wall and began collecting his things. "Why'ja just call me Putty? My name is—"

"Whatevs." Massie held out her palm to stop him from wasting her time. "If my shoes get wet, they'll be done. D-O-N-E, *ruined*! You can have your suitcase back as soon as this leak stops."

"Gee, thanks," he grumbled, as he struggled to carry his ditched belongings back to his seat without dropping them.

Just then, the trailer shook as someone climbed up the rickety steps.

"Shhhh, it's Ms. Dunkel!" whisper-warned Big Mac as she snapped her scratched silver compact shut and dropped it in the pocket of her ill-fitting black American Apparel smock dress.

Putty raced for his seat as if competing in a cutthroat game of musical chairs. The NPC concealed their spray bottles and raced to their desks.

The plywood door squeaked open.

"Is this the eighth-grade trailer?" asked a caramel-blond boy with army green eyes and the kind of deep, rich tan that requires a passport. His loose safari shirt fell across the top of his charmingly wrinkled Dockers, and his biceps flexed when he adjusted the distressed mocha satchel slung across his chest. If Bindi the Jungle Girl had invented an imaginary boyfriend, he would be this guy.

Every girl stared. Every boy shifted in his chair.

Massie turned away for fear he'd melt her mascara.

"Dempsey-doo?" Layne shouted.

"Laynie-poo?" Dimples sliced his cheeks like the blade of a hatchet. He raced over to give his old friend a warm hug.

"Eh. Ma. Gawd." Massie sprayed her face with Evian mist.

"Is *that* Humpty Dempsey?" Claire whisper-gasped.

"Im-poss!" Dylan reached over her desk, swiped Kristen's straw cowboy hat off her head, and fanned her beading forehead.

"Give it back!" Kristen giggle-grabbed.

"Ech-hem!" Massie shook her charm bracelet.

They quickly composed themselves.

Massie studied the boy as he admired Layne's spirited T-shirt and light blue 1950s poodle skirt. *He must be a* new *guy named Dempsey*, she thought. One who also knew Layne. Because the other one was roly and poly and smelled like Cheetos and—

"You were so right," he gushed when they broke apart. "This place *is* awesome."

"What?" Massie snapped. "What is *wrong* with you people? Maybe you're used to living in slums but I'm—"

"Slums?" Dempsey dropped his bag on the empty seat

beside Layne, the one she had obviously been saving for him. "*No*, firecracker. *These* are not slums. I just spent nine weeks in *real* slums, working with my parents in Africa, rebuilding—"

"Um, excuse me." Massie stood and placed a hand on her hip. "Do I sell fertilizer?"

"What?" He glanced over his shoulder at Layne, hoping she might be able to explain. But Layne just rolled her narrow green eyes as if to say, "Go with it, and it will all be over soon."

Massie placed a hand on her hip and tapped her foot impatiently.

"Why would I think you sell fertilizer?"

"Because you ah-bviously think I give a crap."

Everyone burst out laughing. Even Dempsey. And it wasn't a *ha-ha-very-funny* kind of sarcastic laugh. It was genuine.

"Sorry I'm late," huffed Ms. Dunkel, landing in the classroom like someone had drop-kicked her through the door. She took off her untailored green poly blazer and draped it over the back of her white plastic foldout chair. Then she removed her large glasses and wiped them on the bottom of her cream-colored blouse. She put them back on and smile-sighed. "With these trailers in the lot, it's impossible to find parking."

"Um, do you sell fertilizer?" Dempsey mumbled.

"Pardon me?" asked Ms. Dunkel.

"Nothing." Dempsey snickered.

Everyone burst out laughing again.

Even Massie.

Dempsey caught her eye and winked. Massie couldn't help

but smile back, then quickly lowered her head before the NPC noticed. She calmed her thumping heart by painting her name in purple nail polish on the corner of her desk. Unable to control her wandering eyes, she side-peeked at Dempsey.

As if sensing her heat, he side-peeked back.

Then, warning bells began sounding in the alpha parts of her brain.

Reeee-oooooo, reeeee-ooooooooo, reeeee-ooooo. Intruder. Intruder. Intruder. He was an LBR! He might relapse. Don't fall for it. You're on a boyfast. He's friends with Layne. He likes the trailers. He uses words like firecracker. *Intruder. Intruder. Intruder. Reeee-ooooo, reeeee-ooooooo, reeeee-ooooo.*

Massie hit "snooze" on her mental alarm. This ah-dorable but off-limits intruder was actually . . . motivating. Not because of his work in the African slums. *Ew. No!* But because he'd shed his LBR skin in a single summer, without the help of a stylist or nutritionist. And everyone is inspired by a good comeback story.

Even alphas.

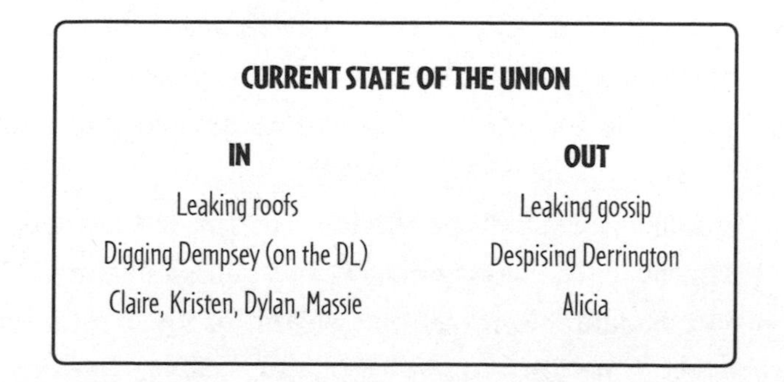

CURRENT STATE OF THE UNION

IN	OUT
Leaking roofs	Leaking gossip
Digging Dempsey (on the DL)	Despising Derrington
Claire, Kristen, Dylan, Massie	Alicia

THE BLOCK ESTATE
GLU HEADQUARTERS
Friday, September 11th
4:24 P.M.

Inez vacuumed and dusted the furniture in the Blocks' spa for the girls' meeting. The two mocha-colored leather club chairs, matching love seat, zebra-print ottoman, sand-colored marble coffee table, and Bean's violet cashmere dog bed looked *Architectural Digest*–ready. The fireplace flicker-crackled despite the sunny seventy-eight-degree weather. And the Baccarat crystal bowls were scrubbed clean of Mr. Block's salty pistachios and filled with berries and crème fraîche for Massie, organic oat-pretzel bits for Dylan, Pirate's Booty and Junior Mints for Kristen, chocolate-covered Twizzlers for Claire (sours and gummies were off limits ever since Cam dumped her), and fat-free strawberry fro-yo for Alicia, which, due to her absence, had melted into a Pepto Bismol–colored soup.

Claire couldn't help wondering if the others noticed the bowl of pink mush—and if the soggy reminder of their ex-friend made them feel sad too? If it did, they certainly didn't show it. Massie's mystery guest was all anyone could think about.

"Come awn, just tell us!" Dylan frustration-smacked the thick armrest of the club chair. "I can't guess anymore." She scooped a handful of pretzel nuggets out of the crystal bowl that rested in her lap.

Massie giggle-twirled her purple hair streak around her finger while shaking her head "no."

"Ewwwww, I got it!" Kristen speed-ran the zipper of her green-and-white Roxy star hoodie up and down the silver tracks. "Winkie is coming over to do follow-up interviews with us so we can prove we're not *special.*" She air-quoted "special."

"Nope." Massie swept her metallic sequin-covered scarf around her neck. After Isaac had dropped them off, she'd raced up to her room and swapped her shimmering gray tunic for a fitted double-breasted black BCBG vest, pairing it with the black leggings and silver ballet flats she'd been wearing all day. She was now a perfect mix of high style and hard business, a combination that confused her friends even more.

"Is it a hypnotist?" Claire bit into a chocolate-covered Twizzler. "You know, to make us forget about boys forever?" She grin-shrugged as if joking, but deep down inside she hoped she might be right.

"I bet it's Jakkob and his new makeup artist, right? Am I right?" Dylan tugged her thick red Wendy's braids. "Please say he's bringing his flatiron."

"It's nawt Jakkob." Massie glanced at the stone sundial above the flickering fireplace. "You'll know in six minutes."

"Or less," purred a woman's velvety voice.

The girls whip-turned.

Gliding toward them, stealthy as a Lexus SC, was a tall, curvy woman dressed in tight black everything, like a character in *The Matrix*. Her ash-blond hair was swept back into a high ponytail and swung like the tail of a prizewinning horse. She wore high black boots and a stylish tangle of pink-gold, white-gold, and gold-gold bangles around her wrists. She was high fashion at its finest—even Claire knew that. Which may be why the crumpled brown paper grocery bag she carried in place of a purse seemed out of place.

"Effie?" Dylan jumped to her feet. A flurry of pretzel crumbs fell onto the white sheepskin rug. Bean lifted her ears, shook off sleep, and hurried over to lick them up.

"Dylan?" The woman squinted suspiciously, trapping her narrow navy blue eyes behind a thick wall of interlaced lashes.

"What are you doing here? Is *she* okay?" Dylan asked her mother's seasoned image consultant.

"Yes, she's fi—"

"*I* called her." Massie extended her right arm, grinning as the silver charm bracelet careened toward her hand. "Thanks for coming."

Effie rounded the mocha-colored couch and glanced at the half-eaten snacks on the marble coffee table. She quickly turned her head, as if simply *looking* at the food was enough to make her bust out of her size 0 leggings. "Pleasure."

She reached into her brown paper bag and pulled out a black can of Rockstar energy drink. "You girls are still in school, right?"

They nodded.

"Thought so." She popped the top with the side of her thumb and forced two orange Airborne tablets inside the sharp metal mouth. They fizzed on contact. "Students spread germs faster than rats," she announced, then took a long, hard swig of her bubbling concoction.

"Ahhhh-Choooo," Massie fake-sneezed, announcing that Effie's black knee-high stiletto boots were the latest Jimmy Choos.

"Thanks," Claire mouthed, not really sure why she needed to know this.

"Not *you*," Massie whisper-hissed. "I was telling *her*!" She cocked her head toward Bean, who immediately abandoned the pretzel crumbs and bolted over to Effie's feet. She sniffed the pointy leather toes on the boots, then circled back to take a whiff of her heels. Once satisfied, she darted over to Massie and nodded her little black head "yes."

"They're real," Massie mouthed with glee.

Claire and Kristen giggled.

"So, what *are* you doing here?" Dylan asked the instant Effie placed her empty can on the coffee table.

"Ask your friend." Effie popped open another Rockstar and jammed in two more tablets.

Dylan pulled her red-and-brown cowboy shirtdress out from her butt crack while flashing Massie a head-tilted, eyebrows-raised silent plea for an explanation.

The alpha clasped her hands behind her back, sauntered over to the fireplace, and turned to face her befuddled audience.

"As some of you know, Effie is the image consultant on *The Daily Grind*."

Dylan golf-clapped at the mention of her mother's hit morning talk show.

"For those of you who may not know—*Kuh-laire*—Merri-Lee got her start announcing winning lotto numbers on the six o'clock news. But thanks to Effie, who hired a hair and makeup team, a camera crew, and a speech therapist, and got her $275,000 worth of plastic surgery, she's a superstar."

"Two hundred and seventy-five *thousand* dollars?" Kristen crinkled her blond eyebrows in confusion.

Claire and Kristen exchanged a shocked glace.

"That's *nothing* compared to what she's making now." Effie rested her bony butt on the armrest of Dylan's chair, then crossed her long, spidery legs.

Claire panic-glanced at Massie, letting her know that plastic surgery, even at half that price, was not an option.

Massie rolled her amber eyes as if to say, "Ah-bviously," then continued. "Once the whole newscast thing happened, I realized we needed something hawtter than hair extensions and more ah-dorable than accessories if we were going to fix our image. So I hired Effie." She twirled her purple hair chunk with delight. "Because if anyone can turn the NPC around, it's her."

The girls applauded.

"So without further ado, I welcome Miss Effie James to Girls Like Us headquarters." Massie led a second round of applause as she switched places with their new image consultant.

"How great is this bag, by the way?" Effie rubbed her wrinkled brown paper sack as if it were made of kitten fur. "The natural color goes with everything and it fits way more than a Birkin. It's going to be huge this spring."

"Who makes it?" Dylan asked, silver Tiffany pen in hand.

"Yorgin," she blurted, as if it should have been obvious. "You know, that albino Dutch designer?"

Given, Claire practically heard Alicia saying, and, for a brief moment, felt bad that she was missing this. It was exactly the kind of thing Alicia lived for—new designer bags, and mystery guests who promised to make them more popular than they already were.

"You should see how many people at Fashion Week stopped me, wanting to know where I got it." She carefully set her Yorgin on the marble mantel, away from the hungry fire. "But I said somewhere in Europe." Effie snickered. "Let Gisele and Tyra get on the waiting list like the rest of the world. I only leak to clients. And now, you girls are my clients." She pulled her blond ponytail over her shoulder and stroked the ends.

"Yay!" They air-clapped.

Without hesitation, they jotted "Yorgin" on white-and-navy embossed Block Estate napkins, with intentions of preordering as soon as this meeting was over. Claire knew she'd never be able to afford the Dutch designer and had to admit that the design was a little awkward for a high-end tote, but she wrote his name down anyway. That way, in two years, when the knockoffs hit H&M, she'd remember to pick one up.

"Enough about bags." Effie cracked open yet another Rockstar, her gold bangles clanging as she lifted the can to her ruby red–stained lips. "It's time for business."

The girls straightened up and faced their new guru.

"This game we are about to play is all about *perception*." She paused, allowing this to sink in. "It's about making people want what you have, even if what you have is no better than a wrinkled old bag from Whole Foods." She gripped her Yorgin and shook it in front of their faces in a *gotcha!* sort of way.

They gasped.

"That's right." Effie dumped out three more cans of Rockstar, then tossed the empty bag into the fire. "See how easy it was to make you think a two-cent piece of paper was the hottest thing ever?"

The girls remained speechless as the flames gobbled up the precious Yorgin.

Massie crumpled her napkin. "*I* knew," she mouthed.

"Me too." Dylan winked back.

"Same," Kristen whispered.

Claire picked her cuticles.

"It's how you represent. Or, *re-present*, as I like to say. We have to make those snots in the main building think your dumpy overflow trailers are *it*! It's *Extreme Home Makeover* to the extreme." Effie tilted back her head and gulped down another Rockstar. "If we do our jobs right, which"—she curtsied—"we will. Everyone will fight to be in those trailers. But *they* will belong to *you*." She lifted her overtweezed brows, silently asking if they understood.

The NPC nodded, assuring her that they did.

Effie continued. "And that is where the power lies. Those

snots will want what you have. They will *want* to be you. But since they can't *be* you, they'll want to be *around* you. And *that,* my friends, is called having '*it.*'"

The girls applauded.

"Now, let's get to work." Effie hurried to the door and rescued her hidden black Fendi tote from behind a wide terra-cotta floor vase. She raced back and handed each girl a brand-new hardcover orange Rhodia sketchpad and a tin box of twenty-four Derwent color pencils.

"For the next half hour, I want each of you to sketch your overflow fantasy. Don't hold back. When you're all done, I'll take the sketches to my team, and by Monday, we will *re-present* those tin crates to the world as the new must-haves for fall/winter."

Without hesitation, Massie, Dylan, and Kristen lowered their heads and began speed-sketching with glee.

Claire, on the other hand, reached for her red pencil and began covering the pages with hearts. Some big, some tiny, most medium.

If what Effie said was true, Claire could *re-present* herself to Cam as someone who had moved on to something better. That way he'd want her again.

All she had to do was:

1. Find a cute boy.
2. Make him like her.
3. Somehow leak the news to Cam.
4. Prove that she has "it."

5. (Figure out what "it" is, and make sure not to lose "it.")
6. Watch Cam sweat.

Of course she would have to find a way to pull off steps one through six without:

1. Breaking boyfast rules.
2. Getting kicked out of the NPC.

OLIVIA RYAN'S HOUSE
FRONT YARD
Friday, September 11th
5:17 P.M.

Olivia's modest ivy-covered four-bedroom Tudor provided a quaint backdrop for the boys as they whizzed and rumbled up and down the U-shaped ramp on their skateboards. Her white-blond brother Andy's rickety plywood monstrosity took up most of the front yard, reminding Alicia of those huge sunglasses Nicole Richie and Mary-Kate Olsen wore on their doll-size faces. It was a whole lot of accessory for such a small space.

If the boys caught too much air and fell to the right, they'd crash into Mrs. Ryan's black Lexus hybrid SUV. If they fell to the left, they'd land in the prickly rosebushes. But no one seemed the least bit concerned. Not the soccer boys in their baggy shorts, fat sneakers, and scuffed helmets, or the girls who were snapping their pictures like proud parents.

"Suh-noooozer," Alicia sighed, hoping Strawberry or Kori or Olivia would admit that they were just as bored as she was.

But they didn't.

The sun was starting to set, drenching the yard in magical orange light, the kind that made Alicia's brown eyes twinkle and her skin glow. Instead of admiring her beauty, Josh climbed to the top of the ramp, clutching a green skateboard under his arm.

Alicia forced a smile, trying not to regret having chosen him over the NPC. Besides, what was Massie doing now that was so much better? Getting a mani-pedi? Laughing with the girls over fro-yo? Gossiping in the Blocks' Jacuzzi? Fine, maybe those things were better. But that didn't mean she'd never have them again. She would. With a little effort and a ton of patience.

"Cute butterfly hoodie." Alicia pinched Kori's pink terry sweatshirt, trying desperately to take the focus away from skateboarding and put it on something that actually mattered. "It's Juicy, right?"

"Yessssss!" Kori jumped up and down. "S, did you hear that?"

Strawberry lowered her digital camera. "What?"

"Alicia asked if my sweatshirt was Juicy." She beamed.

"No way!" She raced over and high-fived Kori. "Hey, O, you gotta hear this."

Olivia was sitting on the Lexus, rocking little Kate. "What?" she called, immediately waking the baby. "I can't hear you!" she shouted over the rumbling skateboard wheels.

Kori and Strawberry gestured for her to come closer.

Without another thought, Olivia left her screaming plastic baby on the black hood and hurried closer. Her white linen dress and bare feet were backlit by yellow beams of sun, making her look like a corn-fed model in a commercial for fabric softener.

"What did you guys say?" she asked, joining their circle at the foot of the ramp.

"I saaaaid . . ." Kori stomped her flip-flopped foot in mock frustration. ". . . Alicia asked if my sweatshirt was Juicy!"

"No way!" Olivia high-fived her friends, oblivious as Kate slid off the car and landed face-first on the gravel driveway.

"Olivia!" Cam jumped off the ramp and raced over to his fake daughter, paying little mind to his sagging black shorts and lopsided helmet.

"What? I don't get it. Why is it high-fiveable that I thought your sweatshirt was Juicy?" Alicia asked, all too aware of feeling like the new girl. The one who had to pretend taking pictures of skateboarding boys was fun. The one who didn't understand their inside jokes. The one who had to shout, "I don't get it!"

"Be-*cause* . . ." Kori grinned. ". . . I DIY'ed this sweatshirt. I copied a Juicy, and these guys said no one would ever fall for it. But *you* did!"

"Great," Alicia grumbled.

"Hey, Strawberry, get this," Derrington called from the top of the ramp.

"Hold on." She propped her camera and raced closer. "Okay. Ready!"

With that, Derrington pulled down his olive green cargo shorts and dropped in with them wrapped around his ankles. He was wearing goofy X-Men boxers and shook his butt as he rode.

Everyone doubled over laughing while Kori and Olivia raced to get the shot. Alicia thought Derrington's butt-flash was funny . . . for a second. But mostly because she pictured Massie standing there looking embarrassed. She imagined catching Massie's eye while she was trying to look all mature and serious, and making her crack up. Soon Dylan and Kristen and Claire would be laughing too. And then, after like ten minutes of ab-splitting hysterics, they'd grip their stomachs and ask each other what had been so funny in the first place. None of them would know. And that would make them crack up all over again. Before long, the boys would be staring at them, half chuckling, half wondering what was wrong with them. And their interest would make them feel beautiful.

But then Alicia remembered that Derrington was now Massie's ex-crush. And Massie was now Alicia's ex-friend. So were Dylan, Kristen, and Claire. So there was really no point in thinking about any of it. Right?

"Hey, why don't we go do something different for a change?" Alicia offered with over-the-top enthusiasm.

"Like what?" Strawberry asked, while snapping shots of Andy as he attempted a series of one-eighties.

"I dunno. Maybe we can go get some fro-yo or something."

"Hey, I have an idea!" Josh called from the top of the ramp.

Alicia air-clapped, certain he was about to suggest they head to the mall, get lattes, then stroll past the mannequins in the windows playing "what would you rather wear?"

How could she have ever doubted him?

"So what's your big idea?" She smiled in anticipation.

"Try using the sepia setting on my camera," he called. "It makes the picture come out all brown, like it was taken in the Wild West."

"Great," Alicia groaned. "Just what I was thinking."

BOCD
OVERFLOW TRAILERS
Monday, September 14th
7:17 A.M.

Massie kicked open the door of the gleaming silver Range Rover and she, Kristen, Claire, and Dylan clawed their way out as if a fuel explosion were imminent. "Eh. Ma. Gaaaaaaaa aaaaaaaaaaaaaaaaaaaaaaaaaaaaaaaaaaaaaaaaaaaaaaaaaaaa aaaaaaaaaaaaaaaaaaaaaaaaaaaaaaaaaaaaaaaaaaaaaaaaaaaa aaaaaaaaaaaaaaaaaaaaaaaaaaaaaaaaaaaaaaaaaaaaaaaaaaaa aaaaaaaaaaaaaaaaaaaaaaaaaaaaaaaaaawd!" they shrieked.

Gripping each other's arms, they gazed across the empty parking lot, seething with excitement.

"Maybe it's a mirage," Claire offered, shielding her eyes from the bright morning light that bounced off the asphalt.

Speechless, Dylan slid on her Bulgari mirrored sunglasses.

"How much do you think it cost?" Kristen lifted the brim on her straw Roxy visor.

"Six thousand eight hundred and seventy-one dollars," Massie blurted. "We came in a hundred and twenty-nine dollars under budget. My dad is majorly proud."

Kristen and Claire exchanged one of their usual *must-be-nice-to-be-rich* glances. Massie let it go.

It was a new day. Her second chance had arrived.

A beaming grin lit Massie's face like a sunrise. "Let's go!"

Without another word, the girls whipped off their strappy

wedges, scooped them up, and raced toward their new classroom. They stomped over tiny pebbles and black oil dribbles and flattened gum wads without the slightest concern for their pumice-stone pedicures. Because they weren't just running for their lives—they were running for their *social* lives. And nothing was more motivating than *that*.

For a split second, Massie thought she heard Alicia panting, begging them to "wait up" as she lagged behind. But she shook the old voice from her mind, increased her speed, and ran past the memory. In fact, she ran past them all; ex-friends, ex-crushes, ex–bomb shelters, ex–main buildings, ex-cafés, and her ex–alpha status. From this moment on, the past was done.

"It's a miracle," Claire huffed when they arrived at the trailers.

The dingy white crates had been painted robin's egg blue. They were wrapped in giant white satin bows, and the words TIFFANY & CO. were stamped on the side in black block letters. They looked exactly like the jewelry store's famed boxes—only a billion times bigger.

"It's puuur-fect." Dylan fanned her pits.

Kristen bounced on the balls of her bare feet and air-clapped. "We should enter it as a float in the Macy's Thanksgiving parade."

Massie dabbed her misting eyes with the corner of her brown metallic pin-striped halter dress. "It's ex-actly how I sketched it. I awnestly can't believe—" Her new iPhone vibrated. She thumbed the touch screen and retrieved her new text message.

Effie: U like?

Massie: Luv! Like x 1000! thx!!!!!!!!!!!

Effie: Go inside.

Massie: Bout 2.

She clapped her phone shut. "Let's check out the in—" Her cell vibrated again.

Effie: Cute dress btw. Love the shimmer pinstripes. Who makes it?

"What?" Massie searched the thin gray branches of the surrounding trees, as if Effie might be perched on a limb petting a squirrel with one hand and texting with the other.

Effie: Roof.

Massie turned toward BOCD's sprawling stone Main Building and looked up. "Ehmagawd!" Effie, looking like the letter *L* in a size-eight font, was dressed in all-black, waving binoculars over her head, *rescue-me* style.

Massie: ?????

Effie: Making sure everything goes right.

Massie: Thx :) . . . going in now.

Effie: N-joy.

"Sandals on," Massie ordered, leading the NPC up the ruby red velvet–covered staircase.

Claire wobbled slightly as she fastened her yellow Marc Jacobs wedges. She grabbed the plush banister to steady herself. "It feels just like the inside of the boxes our charm bracelets came in."

"That was the whole point." Massie reached for the bumpy, white glitter–covered door handle. "Aren't you happy I made you cute today?"

Claire glanced down at the Trust Fund green lace Juicy blouse and dark cropped Hudsons Massie had Inez deliver to the guesthouse that morning. "Totally."

"I *always* look cute." Dylan grabbed the hem of her yellow-and-white daisy-covered luau dress and giggle-rushed past Claire.

"Not as cute as me." Kristen slapped the butt of her gold C&C woven romper and charged past them both. "Open it!" She stomped her bronze Roman sandaled–foot impatiently.

Massie turned the coarse handle. "Here. It. *Isn't*." She giggled while the others bashed into her back.

"Come awn!" they urged.

But Massie wanted to linger in this hope-zone a little while longer, just in case disappointment was waiting on the other side of the semi-glossed blue door.

"Hurry." Kristen flapped her hands, dribbling invisible basketballs. "The LBRs will be here in a few minutes. And you said you wanted to see it before—"

"Okay, okay."

Massie took a deep breath. Opened the door. Stepped inside. Then exhaled.

"Eh. Ma. Gaaaaaaaaaaaaaaaaaaaaaaaaaaaaaaaaaaaaaaaa
aaaaaaaaaaaaaaaaaaaaaaaaaaaaaaaaaaaaaaaaaaaaaaaaaaaaaa
aaaaaaaaaaaaaaaaaaaaaaaaaaaaaaaaaaaaaaaaaaaaaaaaaaaaaa
aaaaaaaaaaaaaaaaaaaaaaaaaaaaaaaaaaaaaaaaaaaaaaaaad!"

Every surface had been covered in something shimmery, which reflected sunlight-soaked kisses in their eyes. White fluffy cotton covered the walls, and red velvet lined the ceiling and floors.

"This is how diamonds must feel all the time," Claire gushed.

"Yup." Massie sparkled.

"It's so cashmere-ic." Dylan rushed past her and hugged the luxurious walls.

"And these are sooo gem-tastic." Kristen marveled at the three rows of mirrored desks that gleamed like unclasped tennis bracelets.

"Lift the top." Massie bit her lower lip in anticipation.

"Ehmagawd, it's a vanity," Kristen said to her reflection. "And look at the chairs!"

Everyone slid into padded white recliners—inspired by the massage pedicure chairs at Golden Nails—and flipped open their desks, locking the tops in a vertical position with the silver hook. Inside the velvet-lined cubbies were solar cell phone chargers and metallic mesh makeup caddies stuffed with Sephora products.

Massie scanned the inventory.

- Sugar Travel Tan face bronzer
- L'Occitane 100 percent pure shea butter hand cream
- DuWop Lip Venom
- Lancôme's Juicy Tubes (Cherry Burst, Copper Cabana, Exotic Kiss, and Dreamsicle)
- 1 oz. petite perfumes (Prada, Bobbi Brown's Beach, Kiehl's Cucumber Oil, and Chanel Mademoiselle)
- Frédéric Fekkai glossing hair cream
- Evian face mist

It was all there.

"The boys' desks are stocked with Gatorade, Axe deodorant, Axe body spray, Altoids, and Crest Whitestrips," she announced.

"Sooo awesome," Kristen said to the mirrored cutouts of stars and moons and snowflakes that hung from the ceiling on thin iridescent threads known to fashion insiders as Lurex. "*I* sketched that. And here it is. I can't believe it." She twirled like a kid in a Christmas blizzard, mesmerized by the light reflecting off her mobile and onto the cotton-covered walls.

"This was my idea." Claire knocked the white, wall-mounted dry-erase board that replaced the ugly green chalkboard. "Instead of chalk, Ms. Dunkel can use these." She held up a bouquet of bright-colored markers.

"Love it!" Massie air-clapped.

"This was all me!" Dylan shouted from the back of the class, where a row of sixteen matching brown-and-gold monogrammed Louis Vuitton suitcases were mounted on iron hooks. "Say hello to our new lockers." She sniffed the leather. "Effie got them from my mom's travel closet at the studio."

"What *is* this?" an enraged girl's voice hollered from the doorway.

The NPC whip-turned their heads, dying to know who could possibly take issue with such perfection.

Layne, wearing a denim bucket hat and an orange DIY T-shirt dress that said TRAILER PRIDE kicked the cotton wall with her black MBTs, leaving behind a muddy round footprint. "How could you *do* this?"

"Do *what*?" Massie shut her vanity and stood. Was Layne Abeley seriously serious? Was it possible she didn't absolutely ah-dore the makeover? Or was this her attempt at humor? Either way, Massie had no tolerance for anything short of praise and worship.

"Meena, Heather, Dempsey, come see this atrocity," Layne called, her slitty green eyes targeting Massie.

"Layne, are you a diaper?"

"No!" she snapped.

"Then why are you so pissed?"

The NPC cracked up from their vibrating white massage chairs.

"I'll tell you why." Layne shot Claire a *whose-side-are-you-on* scowl as she marched by. Stopping in front of Massie's desk, she leaned forward until they were practically bumping eyelashes. Her breath smelled like maple syrup. "We were part of something raw and groundbreaking. We were outcasts.

Educational outlaws. Pioneers! Charged with rebuilding and redefining school as we know it. And in one weekend, you came along and made us Main Building again. These trailers belonged to the people! They weren't *yours* to make over. We should have voted."

"Puh-lease." Massie waved her away like stinky spray-tan fumes.

They were interrupted by the quick hiss of a room deodorizer that shot a hydrating burst of vanilla mineral water every seven minutes.

"Oh, I'm sure the asthmatics are gonna love *that.*" Layne scribbled a note on her spiral flip-top Hello Kitty pad.

Massie clenched her fists, trying to quell her thumping heartbeat, which pounded rage into every part of her body and made her palms itch. How dare Layne be anything but grateful? How dare she stand there and—

"Who called Ty Pennington?" chuckled Dempsey as he stomped up the steps in his rugged, unlaced, worn-out work boots. "This place is . . ." He paused, searching for the right word.

Layne and Massie watched him with unwavering focus, like courtroom opponents, waiting for the judge's final verdict.

"Wow!" He kissed his golden brown fingers and winked at Massie.

Her cheeks warmed. She quickly turned away to swat a fly that wasn't there so no one would see her blush.

"You *like* it?" Layne stormed toward the exit, which was now crowded with curious LBRs.

"Totally." Dempsey's voice screeched with certainty. "I learned a lot about transformation and self-improvement over the sum—"

"Spare me." Layne shoulder-nudged him and a few of the LBRs on her way out. "Prrooooootest!" she shouted, stomping down the stairs and shaking the trailer. "Who's with meeeee????"

Meena and Heather were the only two who answered. The rest of the LBRs burst through the doorway with force.

They squealed and gushed and gasped and oooohed and ahhhhed and touched and poked and whooped with delight. Outside, masses of Main Building girls gathered, snapping cell-phone pictures and envy-whispering. Layne and Meena and Heather tried to force petitions in front of their faces, but the MB-ers refused to sign. They were too overwhelmed to do anything but stare.

A familiar buzz tickled the bottoms of Massie's feet. It was her inner alpha-meter. And it was vibrating maximum intensity to let her know she had reached MAP (Maximum Alpha Potential). *Finally*.

"Who wants to see what we did to the inside?" she shouted from the open window. Dozens of MB-ers flocked to the steps, hoping to get a glimpse before the first-period bell rang.

Seconds later, the trailer was filled with yet another round of squeals and gushes and gasps and ooohs and ahhhhs. But it was the people who weren't there whom Massie noticed most.

Alicia, Derrington, Josh, Cam, Plovert, Kemp—the ones

who needed to know she was back and more fabulous than ever. Where were *they*?

Another incoming text message hummed on Massie's iPhone.

Effie: Get them out! ASAP!

Massie: Huh?

Effie: Make them want access. Then deny it. They will want what they can't have. Hurry!

Massie snapped her phone shut. "All nonmembers must get out!" she shouted. "We have some secret overflow business to attend to."

Dylan, Kristen, and Claire immediately herded the MB-ers toward the door. And before long, the LBRs were helping.

Once the MB-ers had cleared out, Massie sat and gazed out at her cotton-filled kingdom. Something was off. The room was flawless. Her friends were by her side. And the LBRs worshipped her again. So what *was* it???

Her amber eyes scanned the three rows of mirrored desks, bumping and rolling over every poorly dressed body that occupied them until it struck her. The LBRs, with their limp hair, dull complexions, and drab garage-sale wardrobes, clashed in this environment. They were Zales earrings in Tiffany boxes.

After a quick round of text messages, Massie stood. "LBRs, listen up."

Everyone turned to their leader, anxious to know what she had in store for them next.

"Um, excuse me." Great White tucked a dirty blond strand of oily hair behind her ear, her wide-set shark eyes blinking nervously. "What's an LBR?"

It was obvious from the sudden silence that many others had the same question.

The NPC giggled into their palms. Massie struggled to keep a straight face.

"Look at your desk."

Great White, Twizzler, Big Mac, Braille Bait, Powder, Monkey Paws, Blond Lincoln, Bag Hag, Candy Corn, Putty, Dempsey, and Loofah lowered their heads and gazed at their reflections in the mirror.

"Not *you*, Dempsey." Massie stopped the caramel-colored blond just in time. "Not anymore."

He lifted his army green eyes and dimple-smiled, "Thank you," even though he had no clue what he was thanking her for.

Massie batted, "You're welcome," with her Lancôme lashes.

"Now what?" Great White asked.

Massie refocused. "See that?"

"What? My *face*?" Her sparse light brows lowered in confusion.

The NPC giggled harder.

"Yup, your face." Massie fought her twitching lips. "*That's* an LBR."

Great White, Twizzler, Big Mac, Braille Bait, Powder, Monkey Paws, Blond Lincoln, Bag Hag, Candy Corn, Putty, and Loofah exchanged confused glances.

The NPC exploded into a collective cackle.

"But don't worry," she assured her subjects. "I can help."

Their mouths hung open, salivating for whatever it was she had to offer.

"Tonight . . ." She pushed back the bell sleeves on her brown metallic pin-striped dress. ". . . leave your homework in your Samsonites. It's makeover time!"

They cheered with uninhibited glee while Massie slumped back in her cushy seat. Programming her chair to vibrate, she shut her eyes and practiced deep breathing. Once relaxed, she began picturing each LBR, compiling a hair, makeup, and wardrobe strategy for each one.

Her heart raced just thinking about the amount of work that lay ahead. Turning trailers into Tiffany boxes was one thing. But coal into diamonds was quite another.

CURRENT STATE OF THE UNION

IN	OUT
Tiffany's	Trailers
New LBRs	LBRs
TBD*	TBD*

*In this particular case, *TBD* does not stand for "To Be Decided." It's code for "Total Babe Dempsey" and "Too Bad, Derrington." But Massie refused to write *that*. *Puh-lease!* What if someone found her Palm? She'd have to kick herself out of the NPC, and that was so nawt an option. Besides, it was a harmless crush. Nothing at all to be concerned about. Nuh-*thing*!

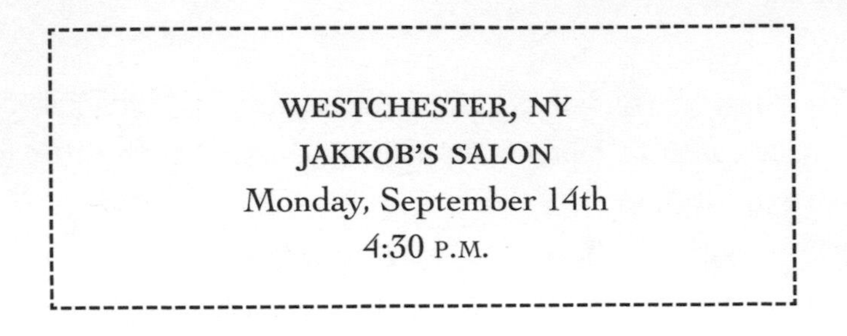

The LBRs squeezed together on Jakkob's round red leather couch in the center of the predominantly black marble salon, studying the makeover spreadsheet Massie created while nibbling on Inez's famous cucumber-and-cream-cheese sandwiches.

LBR	HAIR: JAKKOB	FACE: SIMONE	WARDROBE SUGGESTIONS	NPC: BEAUTY REP
Great White	1. Blond highlights. 2. Add body by layering. 3. Trim split ends.	1. Hydrating facial to get rid of scaly complexion. 2. Eye shadow to make it look like your eyes aren't attached to your ears. 3. Lip liner so it looks like you have lips and not just a food hole.	1. NO GRAY OR WHITE! 2. Bright, non-shark-like colors. 3. Miniskirts to show off your defined calves. They are your best feature.	Dylan Marvil—good with bright colors.
Braille Bait	1. Bangs to hide the forehead bumps.	1.Noncomedogenic concealer. 2. Noncomedogenic foundation. 3. Noncomedogenic blush. 4. Mascara. 5. Smile. ☺	1. NO RED OR PURPLE. It draws attention to the pink splotches on your skin. 2. Pastels would be best. 3. Skinny jeans, ballet flats, and empire tops. This will flatter your thin legs and hide the little roll of fat that hangs over your leggings.	Kristen Gregory—sweats often during soccer practice, so prone to breakouts. Good with pore cleansing and dressing to distract from zits.

LBR	HAIR: JAKKOB	FACE: SIMONE	WARDROBE SUGGESTIONS	NPC: BEAUTY REP
Loofah	1. Saw off split ends. 2. Three-hour deep-conditioning treatment. 3. Japanese straightening perm.	1. Skin is generally good. A little blush and some clear gloss are all you need. Congrats! ☺	1. NO BLACK! Your hair sheds. The person sitting behind you does not need to see this. Please stick to white shirts and khaki bottoms. At least until we get this problem under control.	Dylan Marvil—knows a lot about frizzy, unruly hair from experience. (Sorry Dyl, but it's true.) ☹ Claire Lyons will assist with wardrobe. She's a real expert with white (she's from Florida).
Monkey Paws	1. Lose the orangutan-orange highlights (too much Sun-In over the summer?) 2. Go dark blond. No brown or black. Too primate-ish.	1. Dark brown eyes are nice. Features are symmetrical and well proportioned. Current use of blush and gloss work well. No notes. 2. Intense manicure. Paraffin wax treatment, sandblasting exfoliation. Sleep with gloves oozing Vaseline for 6 months. 3. Try not to curl palms. Ever.	1. No angora, no cashmere, no boiled wool, no chenille. Nothing that could be mistaken for monkey fur. 2. No bananas. 3. Your body is fit. Miniskirts and dresses would be cute but please shave/wax legs . . . thighs and toes included.	Massie Block—I will run a cotton ball up your legs every two days. Should any white fluff get snagged on your stubble, you and your Gillette Venus will be sent straight to the locker room for a "time out."
Blond Lincoln	1. Separate hair on head from sideburns.	1. WAX lip, brows, sideburns. Once we see what lies beneath the hair, we will reevaluate.	1. Sweats are fine. Track suits are nawt! Please stick to the following brands: Juicy Splendid, Puma, Ed Hardy, and Primp.	Kristen Gregory—she has no major facial hair issue (none of us do, thank Gawd!) but she *does* know sweats.

LBR	HAIR: JAKKOB	FACE: SIMONE	WARDROBE SUGGESTIONS	NPC: BEAUTY REP
Bag Hag	1. Your short brown pixie cut is actually kind of cute in a French model sort of way.	1. Your complexion is clear. Your green eyes are bright. Your lips are full and nicely stained. (That's Fresh's Dahlia, right?)	1. PLEASE STOP BRINGING YOUR BOOKS AND BELONGINGS TO SCHOOL IN PLASTIC BAGS FROM CVS AND RALPH'S. 2. Use the Louis Vuitton suitcase we have provided at all times. If that is too big for daily use, please consult with your beauty rep for a donation. Or visit bagborroworsteal.com and sign up to rent designer bags that will be delivered straight your home. They are discreet.	Dylan Marvil—has great handbags. So does her mother, and she never notices when one or two go missing (e.g,. the red Birkin, black Fendi Spy bag, quilted Marc Jacobs in turquoise and lavender . . . ha! ha!).
Big Mac	1. Break up goth black hair with light brown highlights. Add flirty layers around the face to prove the existence of cheekbones.	1. Wash your face. Then wash it again. Then once more. Repeat. 2. Stick to one color of eye shadow at all times. 3. Leave the white face powder for mimes and senile Broadway actresses. 4. Use a small amount of pink blush on the apples of your cheeks. 5. Light pink lip gloss—yes. Red/purple/black matte lipstick—no!	1. NO BLACK. NO SUPER-SIZE T-SHIRTS. NO RED-AND-WHITE STRIPED SOCKS. NO DOC MARTENS. 2. Think Marilyn Monroe, nawt Marilyn Manson.	1.Massie Block —gothbuster!

LBR	HAIR: JAKKOB	FACE: SIMONE	WARDROBE SUGGESTIONS	NPC: BEAUTY REP
Dempsey	1. Caramel-colored hair is too good to be natural. Yet it *is*. Nice going. 2. Please do not cut. It looks great shaggy. 3. Nice transformation. ☺	1. Green eyes pop nicely against tan. 2. Skin is smooth and evenly colored. 3. Teeth are iPod white. 4. Dimples are ah-dorable. 5. Nice transformation. ☺	1. Love the whole safari-chic thing. Stay rugged. 2. Maybe a new pair of boots around the holidays. Something in a brown leather. Kenneth Cole? 3. Body is fit. No more VGG (Video Game Gut). 4. Nice transformation. Please maintain. ☺	Massie Block— I will check you out from time to time to make sure you are maintaining. In the meantime, please assist us in mentoring the boys. They could use a strong male role model. ☺ x 10
Candy Corn	1. Black hair looks cute. No notes.	1. Regular dentist visits. 2. BriteSmile visit. 3. Maintain with flossing, brushing and Crest Whitestrips.	1. NO red shirts until your teeth have lost their yellow sheen. Red makes yellow look more yellow. 2. Stick to navy and black until the problem has been resolved.	Dempsey—has awesome teeth.
Powder	1. Darken your ash-blond hair. Something in the chestnut family. It will help us differentiate your scalp from your face.	1. Spray-tan! 2. Maintain with Clarins self-tanner (good for boys). Eat an iron-rich diet: meat, eggs, and spinach. 3. If you have a choice between hanging inside or outside, always pick outside.	1. Dark clothes only. 2. From now awn, your white long-sleeved Hanes tees should only be used for wiping excess self-tanner off your hands.	Dempsey—has an awesome tan.

LBR	HAIR: JAKKOB	FACE: SIMONE	WARDROBE SUGGESTIONS	NPC: BEAUTY REP
Putty	1. See Powder	1. See Powder	1. Lose 10 pounds. 2. See Powder.	Dempsey—has awesome abs.
Twizzler	1. Hair is buzzed too close to your head. When you blush, your scalp turns purple. Please grow out your hair.	1. Practice deep breathing to avoid blushing. 2. Work on confidence.	1. NO RED! 2. Gain 10 pounds of lean muscle (protein, protein, protein).	Dempsey—has awesome confidence and awesome hair.

After everyone had time to digest the game plan and their cucumber sandwiches, they got busy.

Very, very busy.

BOCD CAMPUS
TIFFANY & CO. TRAILERS
Wednesday, September 16th
2:37 P.M.

Ms. Dunkel casually sniffed the blueberry-scented marker after scribbling the homework assignment on her new dry-erase board. "I just love these." She sniffed again, then thank-you-winked at Claire for coming up with the idea.

Claire smiled back, "you're welcome," then checked to see if anyone had happened to catch the flattering exchange. But everyone was too busy admiring their new and improved reflections in their mirrored desks to notice.

"Now that your makeovers are complete, there should be no more excuses," Ms. Dunkel announced, suddenly becoming very serious. "I want your history papers on my desk first thing tomorrow morning." She unrolled the cuffs of her black silk blouse and smoothed her hands over the front of the matching pencil skirt. Even *she* had made the effort to dress up for their new and much-improved surroundings—thanks to the note Massie slipped in her inbox the night before.

Dear Ms. Dunkel,

I just wanted to let you know that Winkie and her camera crew will be back to do a follow-up story on the new trailers after class tomorrow. So if we all look better than usual, that's why.

—Massie Block

P.S. I showed my stylist your Web site (I was telling her what a great teacher you are), and she said she thinks you would look very elegant in black silk. Her words, not mine. Not sure why she told me this, but I thought you might want to know.

P.P.S. I saw a great black silk blouse and pencil skirt in the window of Neiman's, if you're interested. FYI, it's DKNY. Luvved it!

P.P.P.S. Black silk looks great on camera. I read that in *Teen Vogue*.

Thanks for being the coolest teacher ever. ☺

Claire couldn't believe Massie had managed to get their dowdy teacher into DKNY. But then again, the room was filled with students who had all been subject to a Massie Makeover. And no one seemed the slightest bit insulted. In fact, they looked a zillion times better for it, each one a confident "after" picture, sitting straighter, smiling brighter, and laughing louder than ever before.

"Ms. Dunkel?" Massie raised her glittery bangle–covered arm. "Mind if I make a few announcements before we go on camera?"

"Hmmm, let's see." Ms. Dunkel tapped a bony finger against her thin lips while pondering the question. "Should I let the girl responsible for transforming our ill-equipped classroom into a state-of-the-art learning facility say a few words?" She scanned the rows of students, hoping for some audience participation. "Well, should I?"

The NPC clapped. Then Dempsey joined in. Seconds later,

everyone but Layne, Heather, and Meena was applauding. The three girls took enormous headphones out of their Hello Kitty bags and slipped them over their ears.

"I *thought* so." Ms. Dunkel gladly stepped toward the window, giving Massie complete control of the floor.

Grinning humbly, the born-again alpha sauntered down the row of mirrored desks, high-fiving her supporters like an Oscar winner. A puff of vanilla mist hissed encouragement while the hanging stars and moons reflected golden abstractions of light across her white sequined mini tunic.

The instant Massie arrived at the head of the class, the final bell rang. But no one made a move to stand. No books were gathered, no pencil cases unzipped, no chairs screeched. The only sound anyone heard was the low hum of the vibrating massage chairs.

"Thank you, Ms. Dunkel," Massie started, then paused. She pointed at her teacher's silk-covered butt and mimed the act of pulling something.

"Huh?" Ms. Dunkel asked.

Massie repeated the gesture, this time a little less subtly, like a frustrated charades player.

"The tag," she whisper-shouted. "Lose the tag!"

Ms. Dunkel blindly patted her backside until she finger-bumped into the protruding white Neiman-Marcus tag.

Everyone giggled as she yanked it off and crumpled it in her fist. "Continue," she said with a stern but grateful nod.

Massie twirled her purple hair chunk. "I just wanted to say how great you all look today."

They smile-thanked her.

"But before you walk out there . . ." She pointed toward the parking lot where Winkie and her crew were waiting. ". . . there are a few things I'd like to remind you of." She pulled out her Palm and tapped the screen. "First, I want everyone to feel their hair." Massie petted her sexy side-pony.

Everyone except Layne, Meena, and Heather, who were banging their heads to whatever was blasting through their headphones, did as they were told.

"That's what clean, highlighted blowouts feel like." She paused, giving them time to capture the sensation.

Claire, whose white-blond hair had been styled by Jakkob's famed round brush, fake-felt her locks to avoid flattening her camera-ready curls.

"Hands down!" Massie suddenly ordered. "Let that be the last time you touch. Once you're on camera, you have to act like your hair looks this good all the time. And that means no twirling, touching, twisting, tugging, or taming."

They nodded their consent.

"Next . . ." Massie lifted a tube of Sugar Donut–flavored Glossip Girl and applied. ". . . take a minute to touch up your lips. Big Mac and Loofah, remember, no scraping it off with your teeth and eating it. *We* know the only products that ever touched your mouths before were either medicated or mentholated, but there's no need to advertise it."

Claire, along with the others, opened her desk and picked out her favorite Juicy Tube. She and Kristen both picked

Dreamsicle, while Dylan blended Peanut Butter (one of Massie's GG reject flavors) with Lancôme's Cherry Burst.

"Now, for the boys . . ." Massie nodded at Dempsey. ". . . D is passing around a tube of Vaseline. It wouldn't kill you to dab a little on, especially you, Candy Corn. Those whitening treatments have left you a little chapped."

He blushed and then looked down at his blue henley, allowing a curtain of jet-black hair to hide his shame-filled eyes.

"Take this down." Massie turned to the white board and grabbed a grape-scented metallic marker off the narrow base. Without hesitation, she erased the homework assignment and started writing. Once done, she stepped aside, revealing her trade secrets. "These are the top five rules for on-camera fabulousness."

- Act like you're having too much fun to notice the cameras.
- Pretend perfection comes easily. Never tell them how hard you worked to look good.
- Visualize your favorite celebrity and imagine you look like them.
- Don't ever tell anyone where you bought something. If you get a compliment say, "Thank you. I got it in Europe."
- Sell the DREAM!

The New LBRs quickly jotted down her words. Claire was tempted, knowing Massie had just revealed her trade secrets, but Kristen and Dylan weren't writing. They were nonchalantly reapplying their mascara, like they already knew the five rules. So Claire resisted. But the more she stared at Massie's loopy handwriting, the stronger the temptation grew. Her inner LBR urged her to take advantage of these words of wisdom, for such things were rarely, if ever, revealed.

Finally, refusing to miss out on this once-in-a-lifetime opportunity, Claire lifted her cell phone, pretended to snap a picture of Massie, and captured the board.

"Dempsey, do you have anything else to add?" Massie rocked back and forth on the heels of her camel-colored Dolce Vita platform sandals.

"I do." He stood, his jungle green T-shirt worn to perfection. "How about a round of applause for Massie Block."

He *was* cute, Claire thought, certainly cute enough to make Cam squirm. He was tan, buff, and confident. Kind of like an Abercrombie model, but in color.

And she wasn't the only one who noticed. Massie heel-rocked and giggled shyly every time Dempsey spoke to her. If he could get that reaction out of Massie—during a boyfast—he was definitely the right guy for Operation Jealousy. He oozed "it."

All Claire had to do was let Cam catch her flirting with Dempsey. Then he would realize she oozed "it" too. And before long, Olivia would be a single mom.

"Thanks, Dempsey." Massie blushed. "And thanks to all of you. Now let's go show Winkie Porter that we're not *special*—we're fabulous!"

Everyone stood and cheered as they exited into the parking lot, except Layne, Meena, and Heather. They exchanged a group eye-roll, then a nod, then whipped off their headphones and reached under their desks. Moments later, they were shoving their way past the NLBRs, waving white poster boards that said, DOWN WITH THE MAKEOVERFLOW! and WELCOME TO THE FAKEOVERFLOW and WE'RE OVER THE OVERFLOW.

But the NPC and the NLBRs were too busy *not* noticing Winkie and her camera crew to care.

WESTCHESTER, NY
RIVERA ESTATE
Wednesday, September 16th
6:14 P.M.

Alicia's scalp itched.

It had started on Josh's bike, when he doubled her home from school. More than anything, she wanted to take off her pink New York Yankees cap and air out her hair, because it was ah-bviously thirsting for oxygen. But what if there was a bigger problem? Like dandruff? The Soccer Stalkers and ex-crushes were biking behind them, and she didn't want them caught in a flurry of white flakes. Besides, if even one speck landed on her black cotton Diane von Furstenberg minidress, she'd be done.

So the hat stayed.

And now all she could do was press her head into the back of Josh's gray corduroy blazer and rub it against his spine—a gesture he mistook for affection. Which was obvious, once they entered the Riveras' twenty-two-person state-of-the-art screening room. While Strawberry, Kori, Kemp, Plovert, Derrington, Cam, and Olivia raced to claim their *own* love seats, Josh didn't hesitate to share Alicia's.

"Here it comes!" Kori shouted at the giant screen, kicking her long, thin legs in the air like a circus dog juggling a ball.

Strawberry and Olivia squealed with delight. Alicia, on the other hand, channeled her inner Massie and acted like appearing on the local news was something that happened to her every day.

As soon as the story about a stolen baseball card collection ended, Colton Hedges, a romance novel cover model turned soap star turned local news anchor, addressed the viewers with a dashing brow-lift. "After the break, Winkie Porter will join us with a real"—he chuckled—"*jewel* of a story about change, transformation, and new beginnings. Stay with us." He wink-nodded as the show's fast-paced key-clacking theme music boomed in THX surround sound. A wide shot of Colton shuffling papers about who knew what, considering everything he said was written on the teleprompter, dissolved to an ad for a pill that stopped allergies but caused diarrhea.

"Ew!" Alicia finger-tapped MUTE on the touch-screen panel. "Does anyone want another sundae?" Her silver stacked ring–covered index finger wiggled above the intercom button marked MAIN KITCHEN.

"All fullllll," burped Derrington, who was sprawled out on the puce-colored suede couch directly in front of her, his muddy Adidas dangling off the armrest.

"Very nice." Josh leaned forward and smacked his buddy's head. He apologized to Alicia with an eye-roll on behalf of his snickering friend.

"S'okay," she mouthed and meant it. Which was weird, considering Dylan's whole word-burping thing had been one of her pet peeves since forever. But it was different now. Now it reminded her of the things she missed.

Not quite sure how to please her new friends, Alicia asked

about the sundaes again. They rubbed their full bellies and groaned.

With the NPC she never had to ask. Never had to wonder what they wanted. Never had to question her role. She just knew. The uncertainty made Alicia crave her old friends. But what could she do about it? Like a mosquito bite, her longing left behind an itch she was forbidden to scratch.

"*Nothing?* Not even a fro-yo float?" she pressed, desperate to make them happy. After all, she'd lured them away from the skate ramp with the promise of a great time. And if she didn't deliver, they'd be *get-me-outta-here* glancing in no time.

But the Soccer Stalkers and ex-crushes seemed perfectly comfortable in the Riveras' screening room, where each guest sat in full view of the fifteen-foot hi-def screen. Even baby Kate had her own couch. Olivia had mounted her between six grass green cowhide pillows to keep her from rolling onto the clay-tiled floor.

"It's back on," announced Plovert, pulling his brown-and-yellow Burton snowboard cap over his elfin ears.

"Volume!" demanded Strawberry from the front of the room. Her wavy pink hair spilled over the back of the couch like My Little Pony's bubble-gum-colored mane.

Winkie's hi-def poreless face suddenly filled the screen. The reporter was standing in the BOCD parking lot, wearing a navy Escada Sport tunic dress over matching wide-leg pants. "It feels like another beautiful summer day, but don't be fooled." She smirked, her berry colored lips pursing together ever so slightly. "Fall is fast approaching, and with that comes change. And no one knows more about that than the handful of students who managed to turn those . . ." A "before" shot of the dingy white trailers appeared. ". . . into *these*." The camera pushed past her, zooming in on the gleaming double-wide Tiffany & Co. boxes as if lit by Gawd himself. "Here they come now," she whispered with the hushed enthusiasm of a bird-watcher.

The trailer door burst open, and there she was. Massie Block appeared at the top of the red velvet–covered stairs, then paused to slide on her bronze Dior sunglasses.

The metallic stripes in her brown dress reflected the late-afternoon sun in glittering winks. Her lips shimmered like a glassy lake at dusk, and her side-pony had more sheen than the new Chloé Mathilde shoulder bag. But it was the purple hair streak she casually twirled around her index finger that showed the world how unstoppable she was. Sure, anyone could buy a fabulous outfit, wear shiny gloss, and have flawless hair. But not everyone would have the vision to add a purple hair streak, announce a boyfast, or turn a hideous metal trailer into a Tiffany box. She was always steps ahead. Impossible to beat. The best anyone could do was walk beside her. And Alicia missed that privilege more and more with every passing second.

One by one, the NPC and the NLBRs descended the staircase as if completely unaware of Winkie and the camera.

"Eh. Ma. Gawd!" Alicia heard herself say. "It's a full-awn 'afters' parade."

"Seriously," Olivia gasped. "Who *are* those people?"

"They're, like, almost hot," Kemp dared.

Plovert leaned toward his couch and the two high-fived.

"They've been Massied," Strawberry deduced, sounding one part appalled, two parts jealous.

Just then, Layne, Meena, and Heather appeared, angrily waving poster boards in the air, but the camera panned away so quickly it was impossible to read what they said or hear what they were shouting.

Instead, they saw shots of the NPC and the NLBRs chatting and laughing in the parking lot. Shockingly, not one person so much as side-glanced at the camera. They didn't fuss with their hair, bite their nails, or scratch their inseams. Instead, they mingled and glided from one attractive person to the next with the grace and skill of Upper East Side debutantes.

In fact, they were so engrossed in their muffled musings, Winkie seemed too intimidated to ask them for interviews. Instead, she whispered, the way one does in a holy temple or at a designer's trunk show:

"It lifts the human spirit to see what can happen when the oppressed pull together and fight back—especially when they end up better off than they'd ever dreamed they could." She smiled warmly. "And where there's triumph, there's love," she gushed. The camera cut to a shot of Claire, who lifted a dandelion to her nose and sniffed it. She mouthed, "Thank you," to Dempsey.

Cam stiffened. Kate started crying. And Olivia ignored them both as she struggled to untangle the massive knot that had formed in her multitiered silver chain necklace. It wasn't until Kate tumbled onto the floor and Cam jumped to her rescue that Olivia actually lifted her head.

But all Alicia could think about was Claire flirting with Dempsey. And how she'd better be in the process of turning in her bracelet, or she would sue the NPC for unfair treatment.

"What?" Josh gasped, picking up on the injustice. "That's not fair!"

"I know!" Alicia beamed, grateful, as always, to have him on her side.

"Shhhhhhh," Cam hissed over Kate's high-pitched screams.

It was hard to know if he wanted silence to calm his doll, or to hear what the reporter might say next about BOCD's latest couple. Either way, the only voice that remained was Winkie's.

"Let's leave those lovebirds alone and slip inside the nest for a quick tour." She urged the camera to follow her inside.

The Soccer Stalkers gasped when they saw the rows of mirrored desks, the cotton-covered walls, the velvet ceilings, and the row of Louis Vuitton suitcases. Even Alicia was impressed.

"Who *did* that?" Kori asked.

"Massie," Alicia blurted with utmost certainty.

"I want one," Olivia pouted.

"I want *two*," Strawberry whined.

"Are you serious?" Derrington balled up a chocolate-stained napkin and whipped it at Strawberry's head.

"Are *you*?" Strawberry whipped it back.

"Why would anyone want to hang out in a *jewelry* box?"

Kemp cracked up.

"Seriously, dude." Plovert snickered. "Could you imagine if word got out that the soccer team went to school in one of those things? We'd be destroyed."

"Dempsey didn't seem too upset," Cam blurted bitterly.

"He will be once he hikes up his skirt and realizes he's not a girl." Kemp lifted his palm, knowing a round of high fives were on the way.

By now, Winkie was back in the parking lot, surrounded once again by NLBRs and the NPC, all of whom were beaming and smiling and ignoring the woman with the microphone who was standing off to the side, going on about how incredible the trailers were and how impressed she was with Massie Block, who'd made it all happen.

"Whatever!" Derrington blew a spitball at the screen.

After she signed off, Alicia felt hungry. Not for sundaes or fro-yo but for the NPC. She inhaled Josh's Polo Black, hoping it might remind her why she'd chosen *him*. But it didn't.

What was the point in having a boyfriend if you didn't have girlfriends to talk about him with? It was like having an iPhone without AT&T. A Prada wallet with no credit cards. Gloss and no lips.

Suddenly, the phones in the house started flashing and ringing, all five lines at once.

"What's happening?" Strawberry reached for her backpack.

"Terrorists!" Olivia grabbed her yellow Kate Spade bag, leaving Kate for Cam to deal with.

"Why would they *call* first?" Plovert scratched his hat.

Olivia giggle-shrugged.

"Shhhhhh," Alicia insisted. Once everyone was quiet, she placed line two on mute-speaker.

A nasal woman was in the middle of leaving a message for Mr. Rivera.

". . . I certainly don't pay forty thousand dollars a year to have my daughter stuck in some run-of-the-mill building. Why wasn't she chosen to be in the Tiffany's Boxes? She shops at that store more than anyone. I can promise you that! If my daughter isn't in one of those trailers tomorrow I am suing. And I want you to represent me. So please call me at—" Alicia hung up quietly.

While the Soccer Stalkers schemed about ways to get transferred to the trailers and the ex-crushes made fun of the people who actually thought they were cool, Alicia stared at the blinking phone. More than anything she wanted to call up the NPC and congratulate them on a job well done. She wanted to celebrate with them. Laugh with them. Take part in their victory.

All her life she'd dreamed of *making* the news. Not watching it. And no one did that better than the NPC.

No one.

THE BLOCK ESTATE
MASSIE'S BEDROOM
Wednesday, September 16th
6:30 P.M.

Claire quickly covered her head with her hands and rolled off the giant white featherbed to safety. A spilt second later and she would have been whacked on the skull by Massie's silver remote control.

Standing slowly, she peered across the purple pillow–covered duvet. "What was that for?"

"You seriously have to ask?!" Massie swung her legs over the foot of the bed, slipped her exfoliated feet into her black-and-gold angora slippers, and stomped to retrieve her remote. "Maybe this will refresh your memory." She aimed the remote at the TV and dug her buffed nail in the REWIND button. Shots of the NLBRs and the NPC cavorting outside the trailers flew past them in reverse. "Doesn't the boyfast mean *anything* to you?"

Claire swallowed hard; the taste of pennies filled her mouth. Why hadn't she cleared Operation Jealousy with Massie? Why had she assumed Massie would understand? And why, why, why had she picked Massie's secret crush as the object of her faux affection?

"Exhibit A." Massie pressed PLAY right as Claire took the dandelion from Dempsey and mouthed, "Thank you." It would have been harmless if she hadn't cocked her head to the side, fluttered her lashes, and winked—or if Winkie hadn't used the L-word to describe their relationship.

"It's not what it looks like." Claire tugged the red rope that hung off the waistband of her striped Old Navy PJ bottoms.

Massie lowered her amber eyes and focused on Claire's charm bracelet. The implications raised the light blond hair on Claire's arms.

"That whole flower thing was edited weird. Nothing happened. And nothing is going on," Claire pleaded.

"I hope so." Massie tossed the remote on her bed. She tightened the black satin belt on her Eberjey robe, secured her thick ivory hair band, and circled Claire like a shark. "'Cause trying to make a boy jealous would ah-bviously be against the boyfast. Because that would mean you liked the boy you were trying to make jealous, and liking boys is totally forbidden."

"I know." Claire lowered her eyes and stared at the white sheepskin rug beneath her bare feet. "I would never."

Massie's expression softened slightly and Claire exhaled a little.

"Would never what?"

"Um . . ." Claire searched the alpha's face for the right answer—or at least a hint. But all she saw were two perfectly arched eyebrows that seemed to doubt her very much.

"Would never *what*?"

"Um, I would never try to make Ca—" She quickly choked back his name. "Anyone jealous. And I would never have a crush on someone during a boyfast. I swear."

Claire forced herself to look straight into Massie's amber

eyes no matter how much it scared her. Because looking away meant she was lying. That was how her father always knew when Todd was hiding something. And he was always right.

"I believe you." Massie scooped Bean off a purple throw pillow and kissed her little black nose.

"Good." Claire exhaled fully. "No need to worry. He's all yours." She smiled as sweetly as she could.

"What?" Massie hurried over to her bedroom door and slammed it. "What's that supposed to mean?" she whisper-hissed.

Claire snickered to herself. "I just got the feeling you liked him." She reached for a pillow and hugged it to her body, just in case another sharp object was about to get thrown at her.

"My relationship with Dempsey is strictly professional." Massie squeezed the purple heart charm on her bracelet. "I swear!"

"I believe you," Claire lied, relieved that this was no longer about her—unless, of course, Operation Jealousy worked and Cam wanted her back.

BOCD
ASSEMBLY HALL
Thursday, September 17th
8:49 A.M.

Massie led the NPC and the NLBRs past the row of silver lockers toward the auditorium. They were exactly four minutes late for the schoolwide assembly. *Perfect!*

"Main Building is sooo last year," she said.

"So is this stale lunchbox smell." Kristen fanned the air.

"Sorry." Dylan laughed. "That was me."

"Ew!" Massie expected to hear Alicia say. But a muted giggle from Claire was all she got.

Stopping in front of the heavy double doors, Massie held up her palm like a crossing guard.

"Let's just go inside," Braille Bait urged. "We're gonna get detentions." She thrust her Valentine Fossil watch toward Massie's chin.

"Ehmagawd, are those precious pink and baby blue hearts on the band?"

Braille nodded proudly.

"Then get it away from me," Massie snapped.

"What are we waiting for?" squirmed Loofah.

"We have to make an entrance," Massie insisted.

"Why?" Big Mac mumbled. "It didn't exactly work so well last time you tried it."

The NLBRs snickered. Massie's fists curled. How dare

they talk back to her after everything she had done for them?

"Um, Big Mac, are you a—" Massie stopped herself. She needed her flock to be happy and confident if they were going to remain enviable. Reducing them to tears would have to wait. "Now, everyone, please line up for a quick evaluation. Girls in front of me, boys in front of Dempsey." She smiled as a line of male NLBRs dutifully faced him. His entire face smiled back.

Shyly, Massie looked away, her insides a vibrating Motorola.

"I'll start." Massie spun slowly, then froze. "My gray metallic stretch jeans look ah-mazing with my red Kors flats and white baby-doll top. My high pony is super-long thanks to my clip-on hair extensions and super-ah-dorable thanks to my purple streak. I'm all good." She unfroze, hands on her hips and face at a three-quarter angle favoring the left. She was ready. "Next!"

Dylan stepped forward. Massie scanned her, but it was mostly for show, since they'd had extensive wardrobe meetings the night before. "The electric blue halter looks great with your red curls. Love the super-faded jeans. Next."

Kristen stepped forward. "Love the yellow hooded Capri jumpsuit. Very bold and sporty. Totally you. Next!"

"Kuh-laire, my denim Citizens minidress looks great on you. Don't scuff the orange MJ flats. I just got them. Next!"

"Monkey Paws, what did I say about wearing apelike clothing? Take off that brown angora cardigan and go white tank only. Nice job on the shaved legs, though. Next!"

"Great White, a touch more lip liner and you're good. The green miniskirt is doing wonders for your calves. Great improvement. Next!"

"Braille Bait, ehmagawd! Never, ever tuck in a flowy top, especially an empire cut. Next!"

Massie tingled with pride as Dempsey cleaned up the boys. Side by side, they prepared Team Overflow for their first post-newscast entrance. They shared a passion and skill for makeovers that was unmatched. And it made Massie want to stand closer to him . . . strictly on a professional level, of course.

"Blond Lincoln, unzip your hoodie. All that green makes you look edamame-ish. Next!"

"Bag Hag, your short hair is cute but flat. Mess it up a little. You look like a Fisher-Price doll. Next!"

"Big Mac, a little more gloss wouldn't hurt. Those matte lipsticks robbed you of all your moisture. One smile and your face will shatter. Stay lubricated."

Massie sighed with relief. Her team was ready. She was ready.

"Done?" Dempsey asked.

"Done and done."

"Can we *please* go in now?" whined Candy Corn.

"Yes," Massie assured him. "It's time."

The NLBRs mashed up against the double oak doors.

"One more thing." Massie grabbed the handles. "We're walking to Ciara's 'Like a Boy.' It starts with '*Ladies, I think it's time to switch roles.*' Ready? A-five, a-six, a-five, six, se-vuhn, eigh—"

"What's that?" blurted Great White.

The NLBRs nodded, sharing her confusion.

Massie exchanged an eye-roll with the NPC.

"Okay, how about, ummmmm, okay, Gwen Stefani's 'Hollaback Girl'?"

"Is that a song?" asked Powder.

"Isn't the Hollaback a type of whale?" Twizzler screeched.

"You seriously don't know that song?" Dempsey ran a tanned hand through his silky blond hair. "Even the tribesmen I visited knew it."

"Does everyone know 'Happy Birthday'?"

They nodded yes.

"Great. We'll go with that. Now remember, don't look excited. Don't fuss with your hair. And Sell. The. Dream. Here we go. A-five, a-six, a-five, six, se-vuhn, eight." Massie threw open the doors. Before they took their first steps, hundreds of heads whipped around. Envy-filled whispers hissed to the top of the domed stained-glass ceiling like steam from a whistling teakettle.

Happy birthday to you

Happy birthday to you . . .

Focusing on the purple-and-yellow BOCD PRIDE banner that hung across the stage, Massie avoided eye contact with the gawkers, whose stares warmed her skin like a familiar cashmere blanket.

"Please take your seats." Principal Burns exhaled sharply into the mic.

The overflowers quickly grabbed an empty row in the back. Massie would have preferred something more central but thought it best to sit with her protégés. She was about to slide in next to Dempsey, but Claire pushed past her and stole her seat.

"What are you *doing*?" Massie whisper-snapped, yanking Claire's blond fuzz-covered arm.

"Nothing." Claire's cheeks reddened. "I thought you said you didn't like him."

"I don't," she mouthed. "Why? Do *you*?"

"No!" Massie barked as loud as someone can when an auditorium full of people are waiting for you to sit. She squatted above an armrest. "How about we both don't sit next to him?" she challenged.

"Huh?" Claire quickly sat. "Sorry, what did you say?"

"Ehmagawd, you did nawt just—"

Another gale of nose wind blew through the speakers. Massie sat beside Claire and boiled.

"As I was saying," squawked the gray-bobbed principal, "it has been brought to my attention by several *concerned* parents . . ." She rolled her beady black eyes. ". . . that the overflow trailers are unfair."

Massie looked down the row and flashed a thumbs-up to her people. Her plan was working. Everyone was jealous. They had major "it."

"So we're going to give some other students a chance to experience our fun new facility."

Cheers and applause filled the auditorium.

"She's joking, right?" Massie's heart, temples, and head panic-thumped. The NLBRs and the NPC looked to her for some kind of explanation. But she was just as shocked as they were. And had nothing encouraging to say. She lowered her eyes in confusion and shame.

"Tomorrow night, we will hold a schoolwide competition. Students will be charged with decorating their lockers using the same spirited style and manner displayed in our—"

"Speak English!" someone shouted from the middle of the room.

The entire school cracked up.

"It means we're having a Pimp My Locker contest!" Dean Don shouted, his stylishly stubbled face scratched up against the mic. "Who's with me?" He punched the air and everyone whooped and hollered. "You make over your lockers and local residents pick their favorites. The winners will spend the next semester in the overflow trailers." He paused for more whooping. "The contest is tomorrow night, so get busy. Classes will be shortened so you have time to create."

Everyone jumped to their feet and cheered. The only ones still sitting were the ex-crushes, the NLBRs, Layne, Meena, and Heather.

And, of course, the NPC.

"This is worse than being robbed." Massie lowered her face into her palms. She felt violated and used. "It's like having your brain and heart stolen."

"Kind of how I felt when you copied my math test last year and did better than me," Monkey Paws huffed.

"You went to OCD last year?" Massie mumbled, her face still hidden in her hands.

"Yeah! I was in all your class—"

"Oh, one more thing." The dean swatted a mass of shaggy black hair away from his dark eyes. "Suitcases are welcome to enter." He winked at the back row.

The NLBRs hopped up and joined the merriment.

"No! Wait!" Massie kicked the seat in front of her. "Sit down! This isn't fair!" She kicked it again. "*We* built them! You can't take them away!" Her vision blurred. Her ears buzzed. Her voice sounded tinny and hollow. Was she falling or fainting or both? "We need a new lawyer!" she shouted at the NPC, who were too stunned to do anything but nod.

Dempsey leaned across Claire and placed a warm hand on Massie's shoulder. "We'll get through this," he promised, the sincerity in his green eyes backing him up.

Massie turned her back on his kindness. It was too soon to treat the wound. She had to stop the bleeding first.

"Why is this happening to me?" she wanted to ask Bean. *"Did my alpha card expire?"* The pug would offer her sympathetic black eyes, and Massie would see her reflection in them.

Normally, that would have been enough to motivate her. But this was different. Her sold-out comeback tour had just been cancelled. And a girl could only reinvent herself so many times.

Now what? Dylan texted.

Can they do this? Claire sent.

Guess we sold the dream. Kristen wrote.

And got the nightmare!! Massie typed, her thumbs heavy with defeat.

BOCD

MAIN BUILDING

Friday, September 18th

1:11 P.M.

The halls in Main Building smelled like tape, glue, and fierce competition. Glitter-dusted floors dotted with scraps of crepe paper, streamers, and dented coffee cups gave off a post-parade vibe, even though the main event was still six hours away.

"Your locker is beyond being beyond," Kori envy-gushed.

"You think?" Alicia asked, knowing full well her vision was ah-dorable times a hundred. She'd cut out the lining of every pre-2008 designer bag she owned and reattached the material to the cold metal walls, making the inside of the locker appear as though it were the inside of a massive handbag. She'd even had Scooter, the family electrician, install a little refrigerator light that would go on every time she opened the metal door. Massie would have loved it.

"You're totally gonna win a spot in those trailers," Kori said, cutting into a roll of mauve Laura Ashley Blossom wallpaper.

"Hope so," Alicia muttered, knowing the NPC would have to forgive her eventually if they were in the same class. Wouldn't they?

"All done!" Olivia called.

Alicia and Kori hurried to her side.

Proudly, she swung open the door of her locker, revealing a tiny nursery. The walls were covered in soft pink cashmere, and a duckie 'n' bunny mobile dangled crookedly from the ceiling. Mother/daughter photos were taped everywhere, and Kate was in the center of it all, her head poking out the top of Olivia's book-filled Kate Spade tote. She was crying hysterically.

"Shhhh, it's okay," Olivia cooed as she cranked the dial on the mobile. But all that did was launch a round of hard plastic animals into the baby's skull.

"Olivia, turn that off!" Cam raced to Kate's rescue.

"Oh, so *now* you care," she snapped.

"*What?*" Cam lifted the naked baby out of the canvas bag. A torn piece of graph paper covered in unsolved math equations had been stapled around her butt in lieu of a diaper. He held her to his worn leather jacket and rocked stiffly, like his feet were stuck in gum.

"I don't see any pictures of her in *your* locker." Olivia's blue eyes darkened.

"It's not like I'm *trying* to win," Cam whispered to keep from scaring Kate. "None of us are." He tilted his head toward the ex-crushes. They were sitting on the trash-covered floor, hovering over Plovert and his silver Game Boy.

Olivia tucked her blond waves behind her tiny ears. "Don't you think our family should stay together?"

Cam shrugged. "You'll just be outside."

"Still . . ." Olivia pouted. "The least you could do is hang a few family photos. It makes us look bad if you don't."

Alicia quickly turned back to her locker. She couldn't watch this for one more second. It was like she was trapped inside some lame public service announcement called "Kids Having Kids," about bad choices and suffering the consequences. She wanted her old life back. The one where she had friends. Cool ones.

Suddenly, Alicia felt something poke into her shoulder. She whipped around and came nose-to-beak with Principal Burns, who smelled like orange peels.

"Cawwww, cawwwww," squawked Kemp when he saw the crow-lady. The boys cracked up. Alicia tried not to.

"Here's the schedule for tonight," she said, deaf to their jabs.

Alicia beamed, grabbing the sheet of paper from her talons.

"Remember, you'll be announcing the winners, so dress appropriately." The principal examined Alicia's tight cream-colored knit ultramini with a scowl. "The local news will be here."

The tip was hard to take from a gray-haired bird-lady in a poo-colored tweed pantsuit, but Alicia nodded like a pro.

"What are you going to wear?" asked Strawberry, her fingers stained pink with finger paint.

"I dunno," Alicia admitted. "Any ideas? It needs to say 'journalist' and 'supermodel' at the same time."

"You should totally borrow the navy blazer and skirt I wore to my bat mitzvah," Kori offered. "My *bubbe* said I looked darling."

"Hmmmm." Alicia pretended to consider the nonoption.

"Or that cute black dress you wore yesterday," Strawberry suggested.

"But I wore it *yesterday*," Alicia snapped, wishing more than anything for a minute of Massie time. She'd have had fifteen options ironed and pressed by sundown.

Maybe it wasn't too late.

"Be right back." Alicia hurried down the hall and out to the parking lot before anyone had a chance to question her. She heard Josh call after her but ignored him. He *was* ah-dorable, but sharing every single class with him was a little overkill, no? The magic would fizzle by Thanksgiving.

Puffy white clouds hung in the clear blue sky. Alicia imagined they had been sent to watch over her. There to soften the blow should her plan backfire.

Gripping the banister, she tiptoed up the trailer stairs, removed a gold hoop earring, and mashed her ear against the blue door.

Audible snippets of conversation rose above the chatter like oil in low-fat salad dressing. Alicia held her breath.

"Pass the feathers," insisted an angry girl.

Layne.

"I thought you were against the new trailers," Claire teased.

"I am."

"So why are you decorating your suitcase?"

"This is a political display."

"What is it?" screeched a male NLBR.

"A tribute to the Native American Indian."

Kristen cackled. Others snickered.

"It's not funny," Layne practically whined. "This kind of thing happens all the time. As soon as the little people make something of themselves, the white man comes along and takes it."

A round of high-five slaps followed.

She continued. "Where was everyone during the thunderstorm? Back when we had nothing?" No one said a word. "I'll tell you where they were! They were filing their nails in their dry coed classrooms, looking out their windows and laughing at the soggy geeks in overflow."

"Good point," said a girl. Meena? Heather?

Alicia, being one of the nail-filers, decided this might not be the best time to barge in. Even though she was the furthest thing from a white man, she had a feeling the others might not see it that way.

But what had she hoped to hear? Kristen preaching the joys of forgiveness? Dylan admitting that things hadn't been the same without her? Massie sob-shouting Alicia's name?

Maybe Massie wasn't in there. After all, she hadn't said a single word about Layne's tribute suitcase. And it wasn't like her to let something so ripe for ridicule slide by without a jab or two.

Slowly, quietly, gently, Alicia turned the sparkly knob and cracked the door just enough to peek inside. Even though there were paper scraps and art supplies strewn all over the red velvet rug, the room was spectacular. The mirrored desks glistened ten times more in person than they did on TV. And the white fluffy walls gave the illusion of being inside a real jewelry box. Imagine feeling like a diamond every single day! GPAs would shoot right up because self-esteem would be so high. Gawd! It was brilliant! Massie was brilliant. And soon Alicia would be part of it.

Massie was at her desk in the back of the room, dressed all in white, with her head down. It was the International Alpha's Sign of Surrender (IASS). And it was tragic.

Kristen, Dylan, and Claire stood above their fallen leader exchanging helpless glances while stroking her back. It brought a tear to Alicia's brown eyes. Yes, Massie had kicked her out of the NPC. But she had deserved it. She'd made a pact and then refused to honor it. She'd betrayed them. And it was time she faced them head-on and—

Massie lifted her head and sniffed the vanilla-scented air. "Do you smell that?"

The girls sniffed too, then shook their heads up and down.

"What is it?" Dylan asked.

"Angel perfume."

Alicia's heart dropped to her tanned knees.

"And it's coming from the door." Massie stood slowly, like someone sneaking up on a pesky fly. "And the only person I know who wears Angel is . . . the devil."

Alicia gasped. She slammed the door, jumped down the steps, and raced for cover behind a thin tree on the outskirts of the parking lot. She flattened herself against the back and sucked in her abs. Massie poked her head out and searched the grounds. After about three minutes, she finally gave up. Alicia exhaled.

It was time to come up with a better plan. Something that would prove how sorry she was. If she couldn't, Alicia feared she'd be spending the rest of the eighth grade with girls who thought navy bat mitzvah suits made good television.

And that was not an option.

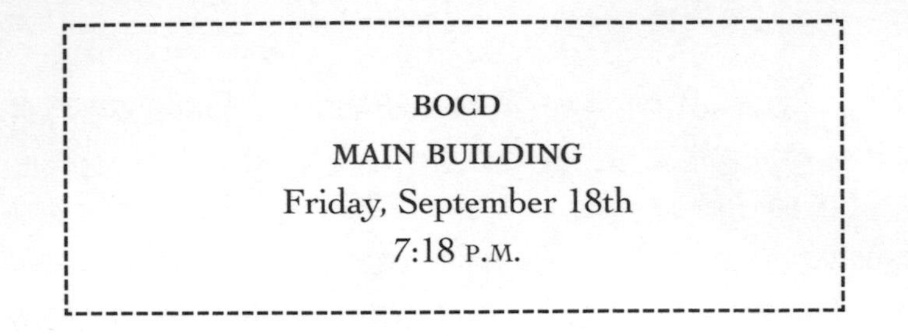

BOCD

MAIN BUILDING

Friday, September 18th

7:18 P.M.

BOCD's halls were packed with Westchester's finest. They strolled past open lockers, their well-preserved fingers pinching the stems of crystal wineglasses, whisper-commenting on the Pimp My Locker exhibit like seasoned art collectors contemplating their next big investment.

Hot white lights topped the news crew's roving cameras, heating the mix of fruity fall perfumes and Elmer's glue into a nauseating blend that made Alicia's stomach churn. Or was that nerves? Either way, the combination of sweet and toxic was a poetic way of describing this impromptu contest, which was bound to end much better for some than for others.

Alicia stepped up to the podium outside the New Green Café, grabbed the mic, and addressed the crowd. The long black lens of the camera hovered four feet from her bronzed face.

"Ladies and gentlemen, can I have your attention please?" Her delivery was part Miss Teen USA, part journalist, just like her new navy minidress with the white lace-up rope ties. "We will be closing the ballot boxes in five minutes, so please have one last look around and then join us in our New Green Café for dessert and coffee, courtesy of Magnolia Bakery, *and* for the results of tonight's cutthroat competition. See you there. I heart you."

The camera swung around to capture the sudden swirl of chaos, which reminded Alicia of the sixth-grade field trip her class had taken to the New York Stock Exchange.

"Great job," Winkie mouthed.

"Thanks," Alicia said with a humble bat of her thick black eyelashes. She knew she was a natural on camera and that she had a knack for memorizing her lines at the last minute. Reporting had always come naturally to her. It was like gossiping, without the whole annoying don't-get-caught part. But still, every time she glanced down the hall and saw her ex-friends huddled around a fleet of decorated suitcases, she felt like puking.

It came from the NPC side-eyeing her. From their matching bracelets. From the fun memories they shared and a future they no longer wanted her to be part of.

While Winkie and her crew were discussing their next shot, Alicia slipped away and started making her way down the crowded hall. There was no question Massie had a plan to win her trailers back, and when she did, Alicia wanted to be right there with her.

"Alicia?" Winkie's smooth, breezy voice rose above the desperate plea for votes. "Wait up."

Gawd! Did they nawt realize she was in this contest too? And that her entire social life would be determined by its results? Results that she would be forced to read minutes from now? But the nightly news was her future too. And last time she checked it was the only *future* that seemed to want her. So she waited.

"We hear there's going to be a protest on Suitcase Row," Winkie blurted, gripping Alicia's arm and dragging her toward the NPC's long foldout table by the bathrooms. "Let's move!"

"*Slow down*," Alicia begged. The only thing worse than running toward her enemy was running. And she was being forced into both.

"Winkie, over here, I got something!" called her cameraman, who was grapevining down the row of lockers, capturing a sweeping shot of the competition.

"This better be good," sighed the reporter, doubling back. "What is it?"

Alicia stopped to smooth her already smooth hair.

"These guys refuse to enter," he said with a snicker. "I think we should show the other side."

"Hmmm." Winkie popped out her shiny red lip wand and glossed up. "I like where you're going with this." She pushed back the cuffs on her poofy black blouse and tossed Alicia the mic. "Coming to you in three . . . two . . . and . . ." She wagged her finger.

Alicia turned her back on the NPC and began. "Not everyone is psyched about this contest." She motioned for the boys to stand up and join her. "Like the soccer stars of the Tomahawks."

Winkie nudged Derrington in front of the lens. Kemp, Plovert, and Josh squeezed in beside him and waved stiffly. They looked like a special-ed class photo.

"So tell us, why aren't you trying to win? Is it the fear of losing that's holding you back?" Alicia asked, trying to ignore Winkie's off-camera thumbs-up.

"No, it's our fear of winning!" Derrington trumpeted. The guys cracked up. "We don't want to be seen in those girly boxes."

"And why not?" Alicia held the mic in front of Josh's naturally red lips, knowing he'd give her a serious, newsworthy answer.

"It's not exactly good for the team's image, you know?" He smiled in a way that was meant just for her.

Alicia looked down, refusing to blush on the air. "Does the whole team feel this way?" she asked Kemp.

He pointed at Cam, who was crouched in front of his locker. "He doesn't."

The boys cracked up.

Cam whipped a pink plastic baby rattle into their circle, then continued decorating his locker with family photos.

"And why are *you* interested in the *girly boxes*?" Alicia air-quoted Derrington's term.

Cam looked down at his worn black Chucks, then lifted his blue eye and green eye, opened his mouth, but said nothing. The leather jacket, worn Diesels, and blue Killers tee gave him an air of coolness that his hangdog expression instantly negated.

Olivia stepped forward. She was wearing a black knit cap, skinny jeans, and a loose black sweater-jacket. Baby Kate had on a black knit bikini top (made from leftover scraps of Olivia's cap?) and a real diaper that had been decoratively covered in pink glitter and dangling threads of multicolored yarn. "Cam wants to win so our cute little family can stay together." She pressed Kate's nose right up to the camera's lens.

"Ew, is that poo?" Alicia fanned her nose.

Olivia sniffed Kate's butt. "Gawd, what's *with* her? I made this cute diaper after lunch, and she promised to keep it clean until the judging was over!"

"She actually promised?" Cam snickered.

"Yes! In her own way." Olivia stormed off.

"Where are you going?"

"How 'bout we check in on that protest down the hall," Winkie jumped in. "I hear things are really heating up."

"Sounds great." Alicia fake-smiled as they hurried toward the NPC. Her palms moistened and her mouth dried as they approached Suitcase Row.

"Start rolling," Winkie whisper-insisted when she saw Layne, Meena, and Heather fighting for Indian rights. Dressed in feather-filled headdresses, moccasins, and Pocahontas braids, they were rain dancing in a circle around a fake fire made of orange and red tissue paper. Their protest signs poked the heavens as they chanted, "Indie in! Mainstream out!"

The rest of the NLBRs had decided to get the message across by handcuffing themselves to their Louis Vuittons. Their suitcases, covered in Tiffany's robin's egg blue wrapping paper, displayed their personal "before" and "after" pictures, while a sign tacked to the wall behind them pleaded, STOP THE MAKEOVER TAKEOVER!

To their left, Massie and the NPC sat quietly behind a rectangular wood table. Their long faces revealed little other than, "We're bored, weak, and over it." It was their standard supermodel stare. Alicia knew it, used it, and loved it. Only tonight something was missing. The gleam in their eyes? Their devilish grins? The sense that there was a five-star after-party raging in their heads "and *you* aren't invited"?

Her ex-friends didn't gloss for the camera. Or show off their suitcases. They simply looked bored, weak, and over it for real. Like subway riders.

"Indie in! Mainstream out!"

"Stop the Makeover Takeover!"

"Indie in! Mainstream out!"

"As you can see," Winkie addressed the camera, "not everyone is happy with this sudden turn of events."

"Stop the Makeover Takeover!"

"Indie in! Mainstream out!"

"Stop the Makeover Takeover!"

Alicia felt like she was on location for CNN, documenting hostiles in a refugee camp. Some of its downtrodden victims still had the will to speak out against their oppressors, while others were simply too numb to fight. It had never occurred to Alicia that Massie Block and the NPC would fall in the "too numb to fight" category.

Normally, the alpha *lived* for power struggles. Thrived on conflict. Refused to lose. This new roll-over-and-die attitude was hard to witness. It was more unexpected than Paris Hilton serving time in jail. Or McDonald's offering fourteen varieties of salad. And Alicia couldn't help wondering if her betrayal had something to do with it.

"Hey, Winkie," she said loud enough for the NPC to hear. "Let me interview these girls. They're the ones responsible for the incredible trailer makeover."

"Go for it." Winkie handed off the mic.

Alicia stepped over to the long table and smiled nervously at her old friends. As expected, they refused to make eye contact. They simply stared over the heads of the distant crowd, letting their open suitcases do the talking for them.

Each case had a round, drugstore-quality mirror propped up inside. The instant Alicia peeked at her reflection, a recorded voice popped on that said, "Hey, loser! Get your own trailer!"

Alicia jumped back in shock.

The NPC snickered. Their mocking laughter twisted Alicia's insides like a French braid. But she knew she deserved it, and forced herself to stay strong.

"Indie in! Mainstream out!"

"Stop the Makeover Takeover!"

"Indie in! Mainstream out!"

She looked into the camera.

"Meet Massie Block, Dylan Marvil, Kristen Gregory, and Claire Lyons, the ah-mazing girls who created the ah-dorable Tiffany trailers that everyone is competing for here tonight. Tell us, how did you come up with such a cute idea?" Alicia turned to face the NPC.

But . . . they were gone.

She could hear their faint giggles rising up from under the table.

"Uh," Alicia stammered, "seems like they want the art to speak for itself." Suddenly all four suitcases bleated, "Hey, loser!" over and over and over.

The words were rocks, and she was standing in the town square getting pelted and publicly shamed. Tears pinched the backs of her eyes. And her tongue felt swollen. "Uh . . ."

"Indie in! Mainstream out!"

"Stop the Makeover Takeover!"

"Indie in! Mainstream out!"

"Cut!" called Winkie, sensing Alicia's dismay.

The light above the camera dimmed.

"Sorry."

"Take a minute." Winkie smiled kindly. "We'll go set up in the New Green Café and meet you there in three. It's almost time to announce the winners."

"'Kay, thanks," Alicia mumbled, avoiding her mentor's understanding brown eyes.

But now what? She stood frozen in front of the NPC's table, surrounded by protesting wannabe-Indians and shackled NLBRs, unsure of what to do next. All she knew was that she had to do something spectacular if she wanted her friends back. But what?

"High-five!" Dempsey lifted his handcuffed hand and hurried over to the table, dragging his Louis like a ball and chain. "That was awesome!"

The NPC lifted themselves out from under the table, giggling triumphantly. Massie raced to meet Dempsey's palm but missed. They cracked up and tried again.

"Sorry, I can't high-five with my left hand." Dempsey blushed sweetly.

"Use your right." Massie blushed back, her palm drawn and ready.

OMG! Were they flirting?

Dempsey raised his arm. Suitcase swinging, his hand finally met hers with a bold slap. They cracked up all over again.

What about the boyfast? Was this legal? Was this FAIR?

"Gawd, I'm sorry, okay?" Alicia blurted. "I want to be friends again. What do you want me to do? Just tell me and I'll do it!"

"Indie in! Mainstream out!"

"Stop the Makeover Takeover!"

"Indie in! Mainstream out!"

The girls stared back at her, grinning, ah-bviously getting pleasure from her trembling voice and shaking hands. But Alicia refused to move. Refused to dry the tear snaking down her cheek. Maybe if Massie knew how upset she was, they'd take pity on her and—

Suddenly, something landed on her head.

She whipped around and came face-to-face with Josh.

"Someone found it in the bushes outside," he muttered, his thick dark brows knit with suspicion.

"Really?" Alicia removed the pink New York Yankees cap and adjusted her hair. "Um, it must have blown off on the way in here," she lied. But come awn! Did he seriously expect her to wear that thing on camera? In front of the NPC? On a Friday night?

Alicia bit her bottom lip and side-glanced at Massie. In the old days, they would have cracked up if she got busted for a hat ditch. But these days no one was laughing. And Alicia was starting to wonder if this was truly a lost cause.

"Hey, Hotz," Derrington called from the middle of the crowded hall.

"Yeah," Josh answered, his sweet brown eyes still on Alicia.

"Get back here before they make you over!" he shouted, and then butt-wiggled.

Josh chuckled like a guy who just couldn't help himself.

"Hurry," called Kemp, "or they'll give you highlights."

"And paint you light blue!" Plovert yelled.

Josh side-smiled unwittingly. "I better go."

With a single nod, Alicia granted him permission to leave.

"Wanna know what you can do?"

It took Alicia a second to realize Massie was speaking to her.

"What?" Alicia faced her ex-BFF with renewed hope. "Tell me! I'll do anything."

The NPC stepped closer, obviously equally anxious to know where Massie was going with this.

"Indie in! Mainstream out!"

"Stop the Makeover Takeover!"

"Indie in! Mainstream out!"

"Get rid of the boys."

"Huh?" Alicia cocked her head, not sure if she heard right.

The lights in the hall flashed off and on, the way they do on Broadway when the show is about to start. Everyone began making their way into the New Green Café. It was time to announce the winner.

"Get rid of them." Massie snapped her suitcase shut.

"What do you mean get *rid* of them?" Alicia asked, glancing at her watch. "How am I supposed to—"

"Your problem." Massie clapped her hands twice. The NLBRs formed a single line behind her, their Vuittons dragging across the floor like limbless dogs. "Ever since they got here, nuh-thing has been the same. And I want it to be the same."

"Me too, but—"

"Then make it happen." Massie whip-turned and stormed down the hall.

Alicia opened her mouth, then quickly closed it. It was time to push her words aside and give her actions a chance to speak.

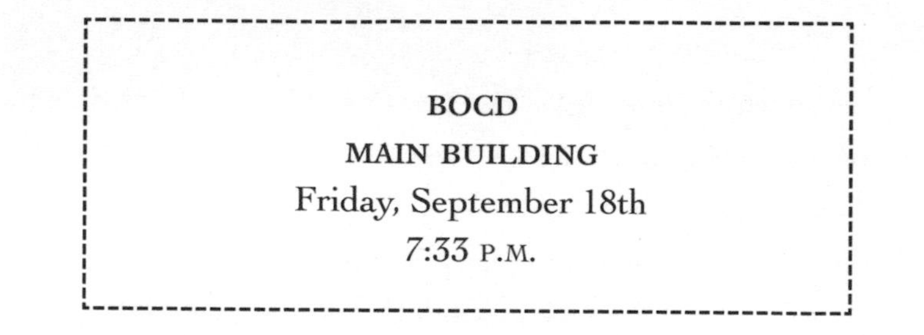

BOCD

MAIN BUILDING

Friday, September 18th

7:33 P.M.

The current of bodies pushing and shoving their way into the New Green Café swept Claire along, creating an ever-widening gap between her and the NPC. Or was she subconsciously willing the separation? Searching for a chance to break away from the negativity that had clogged the pores of her social circle and infected them like nasty blackheads?

Being treated like worthless pawns by the school, the parents, and the kids in Main Building had been humiliating. Frustrating. And insulting. But watching Massie Block fall into a deep depression over it had been unbearable. She was their rock. Their leader. The one who always pushed them to keep going. Without her passion they were lost orphans who—

A sudden cyclone of lavender, citrus, spicy berries, and sandalwood swirled around Claire, derailing her train of thought.

She couldn't move.

Couldn't swallow.

Couldn't breathe.

The cyclone grabbed hold of her chest and squeezed. It itched the backs of her kneecaps and sent a burst of prickly sweat to her armpits. Cam Fisher was near.

But where? To her left? Her right? Behind her? She didn't know which way to run. Or if she even wanted to.

"Hey," he mumbled shyly.

He was beside her on the right, the sleeve of his leather jacket rubbing against the side of her Gap denim sundress. Did he realize they were kind of touching? Did he care?

"Hey," Claire managed, accidentally making direct contact with his blue eye and green eye. Their magnetic grip held her like it always had, only this time she felt trapped, not admired. Like she had been busted for trespassing on private property. Property that belonged to an Ashlee Simpson wannabe who was smart enough not to spy on him and accuse him of liking another girl.

Every day she convinced herself that she was better off without him. Because if he could like a girl like Olivia, he didn't deserve her anyway. Besides, his hair needed a trim. His friends were immature. His one blue eye and one green eye were distracting. His Drakkar Noir was bad for the environment. And his leather jacket smelled like sushi.

But at this very moment, as the crowd squeezed by, it didn't matter what Claire told herself. None of it was true. The truth was in the invisible waves passing between them. And those waves said, "I miss you."

The tears came. Fast and hot.

Without a single word, Claire turned and fought her way through the crowd. She ran down the halls and didn't stop until she was completely alone.

Barely aware of the cold metal against her back, she

slid down a wall of lockers and surrendered to her erupting emotions. Snot-filled sobs heaved out of her. Her vision blurred and her temples throbbed as she cried for herself and Cam and Alicia and Josh and Massie and Derrington and the NLBRs and Layne and the trailers and the bomb shelter and the at-one-time-fabulous Pretty Committee. All the things the eighth grade was supposed to be. And all the things it wasn't.

Once all salt had been drained from her heaving body, Claire felt limp.

She dried her eyes on the hem of her dress. But the crying didn't stop. Loud, muffled shrieks echoed through the empty halls. Claire pushed herself up to stand.

Her rubber-soled red Keds squeaked and echoed as she raced down the empty halls. The crying got louder. More desperate. Claire sped up, forgetting her own sadness, and followed high-pitched shrieks straight to locker fourteen.

She lifted the metal latch without hesitation and threw open the steely gray metal door. Inside, tangled under a fallen duckie 'n' bunny mobile was baby Kate, covered in doll-poo and glitter.

"Oh noooo, what happened?" Claire cooed. "It's okay. You're gonna be okay," she sang as she tossed the mobile over her shoulder and gently laid Kate down.

The instant Claire ripped off the heavy diaper, the weeping stopped. "I understand how you feel, Kate." She tore strips of pink cashmere off the locker walls and wiped the baby's plastic butt clean. "Better?"

The plastic baby gurgled.

Claire used the remaining cashmere scraps and a stapler to make a cute new diaper. "I know what it's like when someone you love tosses you aside."

Kate gurgled again.

"It's true, I do. But from now on I'm going to walk away from the people who make me sad. For real this time. And when you're old enough, you can too. You can even come and live with me if you want. Because I dunno if your parents told you this, but I'm your stepmom and—"

The smell was back. And not the poo smell.

Claire leaned forward and sniffed Kate's hair. Did Cam's Drakkar Noir cling to the doll like it clung to her?

"I'll take her." His voice was caring and kind.

Claire turned around.

And there was Cam. His eyes filled with warmth. His naturally red lips curled into a gentle smile. His leather jacket unzipped. His heart on his sleeve.

Operation Jealousy must have worked. Cam had seen her on TV flirting with Dempsey and wanted her back. But now that he was standing there, Claire decided she didn't want him back. At least not like this. If he was going to return, it would have to be because he loved her, not because he thought someone else did. Because getting back together with Cam would mean getting tossed from the New Pretty Committee, and she would only consider doing *that* for the real thing.

"Here you go." Claire handed him the baby. "I heard her crying, so I checked in on her."

He smiled. Not in a polite, *thank-you-very-much-for-helping* way. More like he used to. Like he couldn't help it. "I heard what you said to Kate."

Claire felt her cheeks burn.

"It was nice." Cam adjusted the pink cashmere diaper. "She needs someone like you in her life."

Kate cooed happily.

Hot tears rushed to Claire's bloodshot eyes.

"So do I." Cam continued.

But Claire, determined to set a good example for her stepdaughter, forced her legs to turn and walk away.

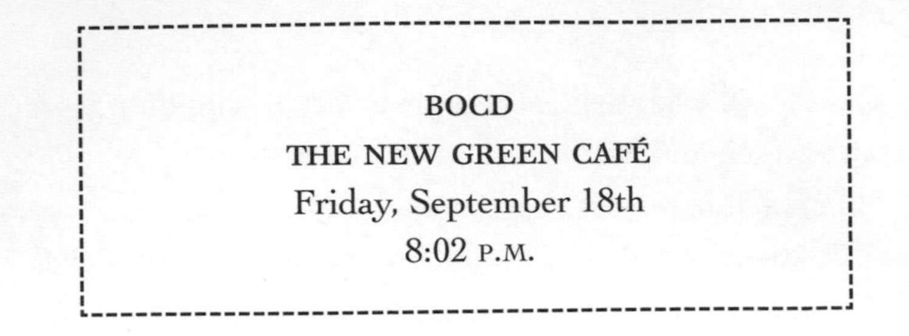

BOCD
THE NEW GREEN CAFÉ
Friday, September 18th
8:02 P.M.

Alicia was used to people staring at her. But this was different.

Tonight, the BOCD kids and their meddling parents had little interest in her beauty, her wardrobe, or her C-cups. All they wanted were the results of the Pimp My Locker contest. And she had them. Sealed in the red vellum envelope clutched in her shaking hand.

It wasn't a fear of public speaking that made her nervous. *Puh-lease!* A cafeteria filled with locals picking at complimentary cupcakes and blowing on lattes was hardly nerve-racking.

Trying to win back Massie Block was.

Alicia leaned into the mic on the podium at the front of the Café and swallowed twice. It did nothing. Her throat was an emery board, dry and scratchy. "And now, the moment you've all been waiting for," she said with measured enthusiasm. A chorus of creaks and squeaks erupted as everyone shifted in their bamboo chairs.

"The new school jewels, who will spend the rest of the year in those wonderful Tiffany's boxes, designed by Massie Block, Kristen Gregory, Dylan Ma—"

"Just tell us who won!" shouted a mom wearing a black

Hermès head scarf and gold oversized square-framed Dior sunglasses.

While the other parents laughed, Alicia peeked at the NPC. They were holding court in the back of the room at table eighteen. As usual, Massie was at the head, with a view of the entire room. Her nose slightly upturned, arms folded across her white sequined tunic, she exuded pure alpha.

From that distance, it was hard to know for sure if Massie knew Alicia was looking at her. And then her spine ignited like a wick on dynamite. Massie knew. They were still connected.

Alicia sent a telepathic IM back to table eighteen that said, *Pay attention. This one's for you!* Then, with renewed purpose, she ripped open the envelope and scanned the winning names. Surprisingly, the NPC and the NLBRs were on the list, along with a few new names she had never heard. People must have voted with their consciences after all. But returning Massie to the place she'd started from would hardly be enough. The alpha wanted more. She wanted her school back. She wanted her dignity. She wanted revenge!

"And the Tiffany's boxes go to Derrick Harrington, Josh Hotz, Chris Plovert, Kemp Hurley, Cam Fisher, Dempsey Solomon . . ."

"*What?*" Principal Burns squawked. "Impossible!"

Alicia trembled, avoided her beady stare, and kept reading the rest of the NLBRs' names.

Gasps, screams, fist poundings, and demands for a recount rose above the jubilation expressed by the victorious NLBRs and their parents.

When she reached the bottom of the list, a lavender flash of light caught her eye. Was she being marked by a sniper? Going blind for lying? Waking from a coma?

The beam was now on her hand. Her wood platform sandal. Her . . . She lifted her head and saw Massie, standing off to the side by the frosted glass doors. She was tilting the purple Swarovski crystal–covered crown on her charm bracelet, scooping up the light and reflecting it back to Alicia.

"What?" Alicia giggle-mouthed, then quickly read off another name.

Massie held up her forearm. DEMP IN MB was written in smeared mascara.

Alicia nodded once. And Massie hurried back to eighteen.

"So congratulations to everyone, especially Dempsey, uh, Rosen. You got a lot of votes." Alicia smiled sweetly. "What?" she asked a fake person in the crowd. "Say that again. I can't hear you." She paused, counted to three, put her hand on her heart, and conjured up a look of great shock. "Oh, I am so sorry. I always get Dempsey Solomon and Dempsey Rosen mixed up. Just to clarify, Dempsey Solomon is in the main building, and Dempsey Rosen will be in the trailers."

Massie was smiling. Alicia could feel it. The ex-crushes and the NLBRs would be spending the next year together stuffed in two metal Tiffany's boxes. Victory!

"*Who's* Dempsey *Rosen*?" shouted Dempsey from the back of the room.

She ignored him and addressed the crowd. "Thank you. This is Alicia Rivera for BOCD saying, I heart you!"

A bony hand reached for the microphone and ripped it from Alicia's clammy hands.

"What was *that*?" squawked Principal Burns.

"Justice," Alicia said with pride.

"No," she insisted. "Justice is suspending you for making up your own list of winners. Do you know how outraged the board members will be when they find out—"

"How are they going to find out?" Alicia tore the list into tiny pieces. "And if they do, just explain that *my* list convinced my dad's clients to drop the lawsuit they were filing against *you*."

"Me?"

"Yeah." Alicia practically fainted from dry mouth. "This whole trailer thing messed them up. They were about to sue you for billions of dollars in therapy. This new list convinced them to drop everything. You can thank me later."

Before the principal had a chance to respond, Alicia jumped off the platform and speed-walked to table eighteen. Her friends were waiting.

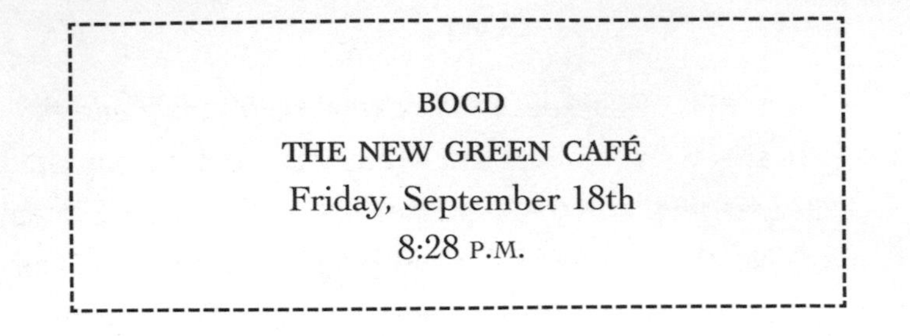

Massie inhaled the chocolate and citrus notes in Alicia's Angel perfume as they merged with the crisp sophistication of her Chanel No. 19. The unforgettable scent of their friendship was back.

Invisible apology waves passed between them as they sway-held each other in the middle of the emotionally charged New Green Café.

Alicia pulled Massie closer; a silent *I'm-sorry-for-choosing-my-crush-over-my-friends-and-lying-about-it.*

"S'okay," Massie uttered, then squeezed Alicia a little harder, letting her know she had been too controlling.

"S'okay," Alicia said.

Satisfied, Massie pulled away.

After a round of welcome-back hugs from the other girls, they leaned against table eighteen and proudly admired the chaos they had orchestrated.

Layne, Meena, and Heather were leading the new recruits in a celebratory conga line around the old-fashioned stagecoach-turned-Sub-Zero fridge, chanting, "Indie in!" The NLBRs were embracing each other, their parents, and the faculty. It was obvious they never wanted to mix with the Main Building crowd again, an arrangement that all sides seemed happy with. The sore losers were being led to the exits by their angry parents, who told anyone who would listen that this was far from over. And then there were the ex-crushes, who had trapped Dean Don against the silver BMW reverse vending machine. Their faces were red, their arms flailed, and their feet stomped, mosh-pit style. And Winkie and her camera were capturing it all.

"Hey, Derrick," Massie called.

Derrington turned, his brown puppy-dog eyes filled with pit-bull rage.

"Are you an actor?"

The NPC giggled. Derrington stared back, his light brows crinkled in confusion.

"I heard you were gonna be in a trailer!"

The girls cracked up and exchanged high fives. This time, there was no question who got the last word. The defeated ex-crushes immediately turned away and continued begging Dean Don to *do something*.

"Welcome back," said an almost-cute girl with short amber braids when she passed.

The NPC regained their composure, dropped their smiles, and assumed their bored-and-over-it expressions, the way the always did when people stopped by table eighteen to compliment them.

"Yeah, we missed you guys," said her friend with the headphones and vanilla cupcake frosting on her upper lip.

Massie thank-you grinned, but on the inside, she was running around in joyful circles. Everything was starting to feel right again, like sliding on her favorite pair of Hudsons after wearing Claire's ill-fitting Gap slim-cuts for a week. (Not like that would ever really happen!)

"You guys look great, by the way," said Allie-Rose Singer as she approached their table, her emerald green cat-eyes wide with envy. "I've been meaning to tell you that since school started, but then you were in the trailers, and we toe-dally lost touch."

"You can tell us now." Dylan spun, showing off her new tight red J Brand jeans.

"It's true, you look so cuh-yooot," muttered Allie's nasal friend Wendy. "And toe-dally skinny."

"S'true." Allie-Rose let the tie-strap on her aubergine tank slide off her bony shoulder. "What's your secret?"

"We're on a boyfast," giggled Dylan.

"Seriously?" Wendy honked. "We should try that."

The NPC laughed.

"Love to." Allie circled her long finger around the edges of her chocolate cupcake, then popped it in her mouth. "See you Monday." She smile-waved goodbye.

"Whatevs," Massie uttered under her breath, exuding alpha bad-itude, as if it never left.

Seconds later the NLBRs formed a semicircle around table eighteen, their faces longer than usual.

"How did *we* win and you didn't?" Big Mac swiped a black mascara–filled tear out from under her otherwise makeup-free eye. "It's not fair."

"No crying!" Massie insisted. "Or you'll go right back to looking haggard and raccoon-y."

Big Mac bit her bottom lip and nodded as if to say she'd do her best.

"She's right." Braille Bait rubbed her forehead.

"Stop that!" Massie slapped her lightly. "Do you know how much oil is in those palms of yours? If you want to avoid flare-ups, stop touching."

"Will you come and visit?" Great White pouted.

"Probably nawt," Massie admitted with a trace of sadness. "But try to smile anyway. Pouting brings out your sharkiness."

"She's right." Dempsey rested a hand on Great White's shoulder but kept his eyes on Massie. Their intense greenness burned her retinas like expired Visine.

"Are you mad you didn't win?" Massie asked, pinching Alicia's leg.

"No." Dempsey quickly lifted his hand from Great White's shoulder. "You?"

"Ummm." Massie felt everyone watching her.

They were probably expecting her to tear up, make a speech about how far they'd come, how many hardships they'd overcome, and how two very, very, very different groups of people had looked past their differences and joined forces to become one.

Like that would *ever* happen.

But she couldn't tell the truth, either. How could she explain to a herd of NLBRs, who just had the best week of their social lives, that the Tiffany boxes and makeovers had been part of an alpha strategy, a big-picture plan to make people envy her again. And that she never wanted to be part of the overflow, no matter how ah-dorable she made them look.

Instead, she waved goodbye to her protégés and simply said, "It was fun. But Massie Block is Main Building. Always has been. Always will be. And I can't change who I am."

A cloud of NLBR sadness gathered above their heads. Some looked down. Others picked their cuticles. But no one fussed with their hair or tooth-scraped their gloss. And for that reason alone, Massie knew she had made a real difference in their lives.

"Hey, who wants to go put their suitcases back in the trailer?" Powder broke the silence, his cheeks aglow with self-tanner.

"Me!" responded the NLBRs.

They waved back at their beloved alpha and hurried off to collect their Vuittons.

Dempsey remained.

"I can't wait to see what you do to improve Main Building. Maybe pad the chairs? Those spa massagers were sweet."

Massie wanted to run her finger along the grooves in his dimpled cheeks, like scraping cookie dough from a mixing bowl. So tacky but so tempting.

Bzzzzzzzz. Bzzzzzzzz.

"Someone's vibrating," Kristen announced.

Everyone checked their phones.

"It's me." Claire waved her rhinestone-encrusted Motorola.

"Who is it?" Massie asked, knowing all of Claire's friends and family were in the Café.

"No one." Claire snapped her cell shut. "Just a stupid text."

"Lemme see." Massie held out her hand.

Claire's cheeks turned red. Massie wiggled her fingers. Dylan, Kristen, and Alicia stepped closer.

"Seriously, it's no one."

With serpent's-tongue speed, Massie snatched the phone from Claire's fist and read the message aloud:

Dumpd O. Wrst mom. U r the only 1 4 me. Let's talk. XOX C

The NPC gasped. Massie held out her hand again.

"What?" Claire asked, her voice shaking.

"Your bracelet."

The NPC gasped again.

"What? No!"

"The bracelet!"

"I swear I had nothing to do with—"

"Uh, my parents made reservations at the club tonight, so I better go." Dempsey smiled awkwardly.

"Which club?" Massie asked, her fingers still wiggling under Claire's chin.

"High Hills."

"Ehmagawd, we go there!"

"Really?"

"Swear!!" Massie beamed. And then she noticed the NPC glaring at her.

"Boyfast!" Dylan sneezed.

Massie's smiled quickly faded.

Everyone giggled except Claire.

"Well, have fun." Massie waved goodbye. "Say hi to Rodney for me. And tell him I loved the cinnamon rolls he dropped off at the house on Labor Day."

"Aren't those the best?" Dempsey lingered.

"Yup. Have fun. See ya." Massie said quickly.

"Uh, okay." He left in a bewildered huff.

She hated dismissing him like the LBR that he once was, but knew she'd e-mail him later with some kind of apology and he'd forgive her.

"Now give me that bracelet!" Massie snarled, her patience waning.

"I can't believe this." Claire slid the platinum chain off her wrist and smacked it into Massie's palm.

Alicia's brown eyes widened. Dylan tied her curly red hair in knots. And Kristen grabbed her shark-tooth necklace.

"Now you," Massie said to Kristen.

"What? What did I do? Is it this necklace? Okay, fine, it's from Dune. But we haven't talked since the boyfast. Not even a single text. He's on an island in the middle of the Pacific with no cell service. And he won't be back until next week. And I can prove it. If you don't believe me—"

Massie rolled her eyes impatiently. "Give it."

Kristen did what she was told, then exchanged a horror-filled *what's-going-awn* glance with Claire.

"Next!"

"Why me?" Dylan screeched. "The only guys I've had contact with have been Mike and Ike. And that only happened once. During an extreme sugar craving."

"Just do it," Massie sighed.

Dylan unclasped her bracelet and tossed it onto the bamboo table. It slid onto the floor, yet no one bothered to pick it up.

"As of this moment"—Massie shimmied the Tiffany's bracelet off her wrist—"the boyfast is officially over."

"*What?*" The girls smiled.

"How can we be alphas if we're not breaking hearts our last year of middle school?"

"Point!" Alicia lifted her finger.

"I'll get new bracelets tomorrow," Massie promised, then got scooped up in a group hug. "Let the eighth grade begin!" she shouted from inside their tight circle.

"Let the eighth grade begin!" they shouted back, living for Monday.

CURRENT STATE OF THE UNION

IN	**OUT**
PC	NPC
Dempsey	Derrington
Boyfest!!!	Boyfast
ME☺	

Want to be **IN** and find out what really happened last summer?

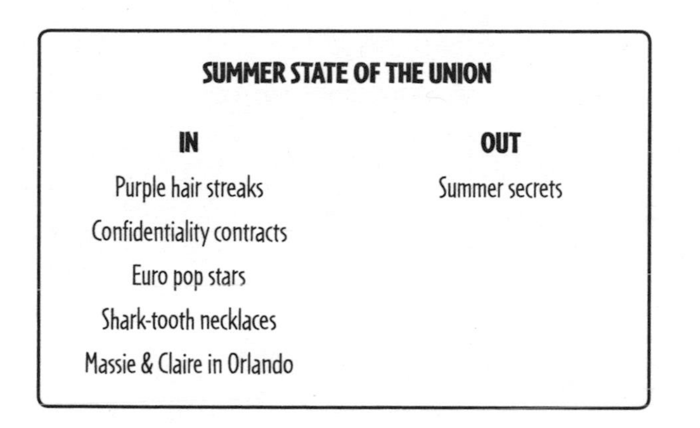

SUMMER STATE OF THE UNION

IN	OUT
Purple hair streaks	Summer secrets
Confidentiality contracts	
Euro pop stars	
Shark-tooth necklaces	
Massie & Claire in Orlando	

Five girls. Five stories. One ah-mazing summer.

THE CLIQUE SUMMER COLLECTION

Coming April, May, June, July, & August.

Turn the page for a sneak peek of Massie's story. . . .

THE CLIQUE SUMMER COLLECTION

MASSIE

BY LISI HARRISON

GALWAUGH FARMS SLEEP-AWAY RIDING CAMP
HORSE STALL A
Monday, June 10th
8:15 AM

The morning sun felt like a spotlight. It cast a thick yellow beam through the window in Brownie's humid hay-filled stall, illuminating the white horse and blinding his owner. But Massie Block didn't mind one bit. She craved it. Chased it. Dressed for it. She was used to the glare of the spotlight. Basking in its warmth kept her alive. Yet today, the spotlight was threatening to shine on someone else. And Massie wanted to die.

She lowered her tortoiseshell Dior glasses and snapped the purple glitter hair elastic around the bottom of Brownie's last mane-braid. His intricate hairstyle, aubergine satin blinders, and gold glitter mascara were sure to impress the judges of the Galwaugh Farms' JACC—Jump and Cantor Competition—and more importantly, the editor of *Horse and Rider*. For the first time in the equestrian magazine's history, the winning captain of the Galwaugh Farms' JACC would be featured on the glossy cover of its September issue. And what better way to kick off eighth grade at OCD than with a beautifully airbrushed alpha-portrait?

Pop!

Massie jumped. The sound of her teammate Jacqueline Dyer popping Forever Fruit Stride gum between her overbleached teeth was unnerving.

"J, can you puh-lease stop that!" Massie hissed at the dark brown wood stall-wall between them. "You're scaring Brownie."

"Sah-rreee," Jacqueline called, her nasal voice slightly higher than usual. "It's a nervous thing."

"What are you so nervous about?" Massie asked, already knowing the answer. She tucked her black-and-gold Hermès cravat into the sharp V of her velvet riding vest even though it was perfectly tucked already. It was all she could do to keep from stress-biting the black tips off her not-so-French French manicure. "Those blue ribbons have Galwaugh Goddesses written all over them."

"Unless the Mane Mamas take *first*," Whitney Bennett chimed in from behind the opposite wall.

"Impossible!" Massie barked at her summer best friends. "We win JACC every year." As team captain it was her job to keep everyone positive, even when things seemed utterly hopeless.

"Yeah, but we never had Fall-a Abdul on our team," Jacqueline set off a round of gum pops that made Brownie's gold lashes flutter in panic.

"Stop calling me *that,*" Selma Gallman whined from the far end of the stable. "I told you, I got an inner ear infection from swimming in the lake yesterday. And that's why I keep falling. My balance is off."

"What was your excuse last week?" Massie marched out of her stall and straight into Selma's. "Or the week before?" The calm, confident leader act was done. She lifted her Diors and glared into Selma's heavy-lidded mud-brown eyes. "Thanks to your *ear,* my six-year winning streak is in major jeopardy." Her voice trembled. A vision of the highly decorated "Wins Wall" in her bedroom—between the bay window and the walk-in closet—flashed before her. It had just enough room for one last ribbon and a framed cover of *Horse and Rider.* And the thought of that space staying empty filled her amber eyes with salty pre-tears. Not only for her. Or the Galwaugh Goddesses. But for Brownie and his elegant hairstyle and all of his hard practicing.

Glancing out the window, Massie tried to distract herself. But the sight of junior campers, staff members, parents, and local reporters making their way to the dirt-paved arena only upset her more. The only thing worse than losing was losing in public. And thanks to Selma, she was minutes away from both.

The familiar smell of Jacqueline's citrus-scented gum and Whitney's flowery freesia hoof 'n' nail cream enveloped her. Her girls were standing beside her now in solidarity, shooting how-could-you-be-so-lame rays at Selma and Latte—her carrot-farting steed.

Whitney scraped her riding crop against the scrubbed concrete. "How *did* you qualify for our team anyway?"

"Not the point." Selma took her pink fleshy hand off her cocoa horse's buttock and placed it on her own lumpy hip. "I thought the whole point of riding was to have fun."

"No Sel-muh." Massie kicked a haystack with her black Hermes riding boots. "The whole point of riding is to win. The *fun* part is laughing at the losers."

Selma opened her heart-shaped mouth to respond but was cut off by Alessandro, their award-winning horse-groomer.

"A good luck gift for youuuu," he announced in his sing-songy European accent.

Everyone turned to face the tall forty-something man bounding toward them in an ivory linen suit and Gucci loafers. No socks. He had four enormous silver gift bags swinging from the mini-biceps on his hooked fingers.

"Enjoyyyy." Alessandro smiled proudly, deepening the Botox-thirsty smile lines that jutted out from the sides of his dark eyes. He offered each girl her bag then stepped back to witness the joy.

Massie offered Alessandro a courteous pre-thank you smile. But it was a fake. Unless the bag contained the secret to keeping Selma on her saddle during the competition, its contents were meaningless.

"Toooo cuh-yoot." Jacqueline held up a delicious caramel-leather saddle with a big J hand-stitched in scarlet thread across the seat. Its dangling stirrups were studded with tiny red horseshoes for luck.

"I second that." Whitney kissed her scarlet W, leaving behind a soft pink glossy lip print.

"Third." Jacqueline giggled into the big yellow bubble she was blowing. It popped against her wide smile.

Massie rolled her eyes as Selma fought to position her new saddle on Latte, the pink elastic band on her cotton underwear oozing out the top of her jodhpurs as she struggled with her straddle-mount.

"Hey, Elizabeth Hassel-buuut," Massie snickered. "Stop torturing us with *The View*!"

"Whoa!" Whitney blurted, just like she always did when someone said something most people would simply laugh at.

Jacqueline giggled into the big yellow bubble she was blowing. It popped against her wide smile.

"Latte's skin is oily," Selma said, defensively. Her shifty eyes bore into the groomer, filling him with blame. "He wasn't greasy *before* camp started."

Alessandro grabbed his long salt-'n'-pepper-colored ponytail. "With all due respect Ms. Gallman, I have been show-grooming for twenty-seven years, and I have never been accused of *oily animal*. Not even during my stint with the seal theater at Sea World." He took off his linen jacket and folded it across one arm, smoothing out the heat-creased sleeves with intense concentration. "Now open your gift," he urged Massie.

"Why?" She flattened the saddlebags on her olive jodhpurs. "I know what it is."

"Yes, my dear captain." He playfully flicked the metallic bag with his buffed fingernail. "But yours is special."

Special? Massie felt her lips curl into a soft grin. She was a sucker for that word.

She lifted the silver tissue paper out of the bag and stuffed it in a hanging copper bucket marked GUM RAPPERS that had been incorrectly spelled by Jacqueline in Paint-the-Town-Red nail polish.

"What's this?" Massie pulled out the caramel-leather

saddle and examined the gold arm fixed to the left of the cantle. She pushed the button at its base and out popped a gleaming round side view mirror.

"To check the competition?" Whitney wrinkled her freckle-dusted nose in confusion.

"No." Alessandro beamed. "The gloss."

"Whoa!" Whitney cupped the tightly wound blond hair-bun on the back of her head.

Massie stood on her tiptoes and threw her arms around him. Her vision fogged—a mix of joy-tears and a reaction to the pungent smell of his spicy deodorant.

"Now these." Jacqueline hurried to her stall and quickly returned with an armful of velvet helmets. "I had our team name inscribed on the back."

Massie reached for hers. Funny how ah-dorable accessories had a way of lightening even the darkest of times. . . .

"Wait." She winced, staring at the swirling red letters that spelled *Galwaugh Girls*. "What is *this*?"

"Aren't they sweet?" Jacqueline asked as she happily handed out the rest.

"But we're the Galwaugh *Goddesses*! And we have been for six summers." Massie picked at the thread to see if it was removable.

It wasn't.

Jacqueline pulled one of her tight black curls, then released, *boing*-ing it back into place above her shoulder "I couldn't fit Goddesses on the back," she explained. "It was too long."

"So is this day." Massie tucked a glossy strand of chestnut

hair into the unsightly mandatory hair net, and fastened the leather strap on her helmet with an angry snap.

Just then Lill, the Head Equestrian, spoke over the camp loud speaker in her shaky old lady voice. "Galwaugh Farms' fifty-seventh annual JACC is about to commence. Spectators, take your seats. Riders, mount your horses."

The Galwaugh Girls squealed with nervous delight while Massie prayed.

Instead of thanking Gawd for the usual—her ah-mazing teammates, their trusted horses, and their guaranteed spot in the winner's circle—she looked up at the dark wood rafters and stuck out her tongue. Thanks *ah-lot.*

"It's showtime." Alessandro clapped. "Everyone in formation—Whitney, Selma, Jacqueline, then Captain Massie in the rear."

"Massie in the *rear,*" Whitney, Jacqueline, and Massie all repeated in a fit of laughter, just like they did every year their groomer called their precession order.

Selma rolled her droopy eyes.

"Chip chip!" Alessandro barked his Euro-version of "chop-chop" while swatting at a circling fly.

Without another word the girls speed-glossed, buttoned their black velvet blazers and reached for the brown suede reigns on their gold-dusted horses.

Once outside, they climbed up on their new saddles and joined the silent ceremonial parade of sixteen riders down the lush tree-lined path toward the arena.

The collective clip-clopping of horseshoes against the

gravel synched with the rhythm of Massie's speeding heartbeat, delivering a hint of harmony to a situation that had been stressing her out for days. She took deep cleansing breaths. . . . In through the nose . . . and . . . out through the mouth. . . .

The fresh leafy smell of a new summer and the familiar bobbing of her A-cups calmed her. Casually, she snuck a peek at the competition in her side-mirror. None of the other girls had coordinated helmets or saddles. Some had pimped their rides, but the yellow tulip tiara on Aspen's oversized white head or a pink polka-dot mane-bow in Lightfoot's tangled locks was no challenge for Massie and her sparkling Galwaugh Girls. A confidant half-smile worked its way up the left side of her tanned face. They would clean up in the style category. And surly her score would elevate Selma's and—

A round of flashbulbs went off when they entered the holding ring—a circular pen with a sliding metal gate that led to the hurdle-filled arena. Local reporters and family members surrounded the rails, shouting good luck wishes to their favorite riders.

"Over here!" called a chubby red-headed woman wearing a white visor with the iconic *Horse and Rider* Clydesdale printed on the brim. Massie offered her a winning grin. But before the reporter could remove the lens cap from her Nikon, Brownie stopped suddenly, jerking Massie forward and ruining her photo op.

"Whoa!" Whitney hollered, slapping her white-gloved hand over her glossy mouth. "Check her out!" She pointed at the ground with her free hand.

Massie gasped.

Selma was rolling across the dusty ring like a wayward clump of tumbleweed stuffed in tight, oat-colored jodhpurs.

A team of medics raced toward her crumpled form.

Cameras clicked. Spectators stood. The Mane Mamas, the Giddy-Ups and the Hot 2 Trots snickered. Massie squeezed her suede reigns until her knuckles turned white.

"We're so done," she muttered, angling her body so the reporter couldn't document her panic sweat–slicked forehead.

"I know what she needs." Jacqueline's wide brown eyes flickered with mischief as she spit a wad of yellow gum into her glove and tossed it on Selma's saddle. "Maybe that'll hold her for a while."

"Very funny." Selma flicked the gum to the dirt as two over-denim-ed female stable hands lifted her back onto her saddle.

Whitney and Jacqueline smiled into their white-gloved hands.

Massie wanted to giggle with the rest of her teammates but couldn't. There was no time. Her reputation, her ribbon, and her magazine cover were about to ride off into the sunset and leave her in the dirt. Just like Jacqueline's chewed-up sticky wad of Forever Fruit Stride.

Unless . . .

"I forgot Brownie's face mist," Massie announced as she leaned left and tugged on the reigns. "Be right back!"

Her gold-dusted horse quickly charged the exit. Coaches and counselors urged her to stop but Massie refused. Seconds later she was tearing down the deserted trail; butt lifted, knees bent and abs tight. Two words propelling her forward—the same two words that gave her life meaning.

They were NUMBER and ONE.

In that order.

Find out what Massie does to get knocked off her high horse in . . .

THE CLIQUE SUMMER COLLECTION

MASSIE

BY LISI HARRISON

After getting kicked out of her ultra-exclusive riding camp, Massie's parents force her to do the unthinkable—find a summer job. She becomes a sales rep for BE PRETTY cosmetics and quickly learns that transforming LBRs into glam-girls takes more than a swish of her mascara-wand. . . .

Coming April 2008

Check out the new and improved CLIQUE sites!

The Pretty Committee is only a "clique" away.